A WHISPER OF EVIL

A GRIPPING BRITISH DETECTIVE CRIME THRILLER

JAMES D MORTAIN

MANVERS PUBLISHING

James Dhht

This book is dedicated to my Aunt Edna, whose love and support will never be forgotten.

A WHISPER OF EVIL

A DI CHILCOTT MYSTERY
BOOK THREE

Edited by Debz Hobbs-Wyatt
Cover design © Manvers Publishing
Images: Peter Wollinga/Shutterstock.com
Philip Birtwistle/Shutterstock.com

ISBN: 978-1-9160084-9-6

PROLOGUE

Saturday 5th March

10:23 p.m.

Madeleine Gilbert waited outside the closed stage side door for her new acting *crush* to emerge. It was a narrow street that ran alongside the famous old Theatre Royal in Bath. She wasn't alone, though. Several eager theatre fans were waiting for their heroes to come out through the doors. Some other actors had already left via the same exit, some of them quite well known to Madeleine. She recognised one of them from a TV series, one of those period costume dramas, but none of the actors had caught her eye in quite the same way as Travis Yardley. To her, he was simply adorable. And Madeleine had a quiet confidence that he would like her too if he was so inclined. She knew all about him, having googled his name repeatedly in the days leading up to the show. He had a wife, but according to a sensation-alist three-month-old news report from one of the tabloids, their relationship had been rocky for years, and now, appar-ently, he was back on the market.

She had been waiting outside for just over thirty-five minutes, and her long dark hair had become drab and matted in the damp night air. She hadn't given the weather conditions a second thought; instead, her mind didn't have the capacity to think about anything other than Travis Yardley.

The outdoor covered seating areas of nearby bars and restaurants were buzzing with people seemingly oblivious to the super-talented cast who were still slowly trickling out through the side door of the theatre. She lingered in the shadows of the wall line so as not to draw attention to herself, and then she saw him.

A sudden rush of adrenalin made her half-stumble back-wards; her cheeks flushing in wild anticipation of him walking in her direction. He was coming closer, and she stood taller, peeling herself away from the security of the wall. She stepped sideways by no more than a foot, but enough to make him break stride and, most importantly, glance at her as he passed.

If a heart could sing, hers would be screaming the *Macarena* at the top of its sodding voice. It was certainly making the moves, and now he was close; she didn't care who might notice.

'I think you're amazing,' Madeleine said breathlessly.

He turned his head towards her in recognition of her comment, and then, amazingly, he stopped walking.

'Will you sign my programme, please?' she said,

reaching out with a rolled-up glossy brochure that had set her back ten quid at the start of the night. She had already turned to the right page, and Travis's face had been staring back at her for the entirety of the show as she cradled "him" in the warm comfort of her lap.

He peered at Madeleine for a considered second, politely smiled and looked beyond her shoulder towards the noisy bar area.

'Sure,' he said, stepping back towards her.

He was utterly gorgeous. Those dark and expressive eyes were cutting right through the little personal barrier Madeleine struggled to maintain between them.

He waited for a beat and then gestured with a hand as if writing something in mid-air.

'Oh, sorry,' Madeleine fussed, digging a hand into her clutch bag and producing a Sharpie pen which she handed him slowly, keeping hold of it just long enough for him to look into her eyes one more time.

'Who shall I make it out to?' Travis asked in his deep velvety tone.

'Oh, um… Madeleine. I'm Madeleine. Can you make it to Madeleine, please?'

'Pretty name.'

He caught her eye, just long enough for Madeleine to know that he found her attractive.

Travis held the theatre programme out before him, and his phone began ringing inside his trouser pocket.

'Thank you,' Madeleine replied, desperate to keep his attention. She looked down at his masculine smiling lips and took in the rest of his face. Their eyes locked together once again.

'Do you mind…?' he said, drawing a circle in the air with his index finger for Madeleine to turn around.

'Are you going to answer your phone?' Madeleine asked him as the caller persisted in their attempts to get a response.

'It can wait,' he said, not taking his eyes from Madeleine. 'I know who it'll be.'

He repeated the twirl of his finger, and she willingly obliged, and a huge grin passed her lips as she felt Travis pressing down on her back as he signed the theatre programme.

Travis Yardley just touched me; her ecstatic voice bellowed inside her head.

She spun quickly back around, and he handed her the programme, but this time, he held onto the pen as Madeleine grabbed for it.

Another fan barged into the side of Madeleine, forcing her forwards, spilling the contents of her bag and brochure onto the pavement. As she looked back, hoping for Travis to still be there, a female fan was forcing a phone camera into Travis's face and grabbing a 'selfie' alongside him.

Madeleine swiftly scooped the spilt belongings back into her bag and readjusted her jacket. 'I suppose that's one way to do it,' she said, attempting to turn the embarrassing experience into humour.

Travis stood motionless for a second.

'It's okay,' Madelaine said. 'I'm okay. I suppose you get that a lot from your female followers.'

'Do you live here in Bath,' he asked. 'In this stunning town?'

'Yes, I do… well, not really. Well, almost. Not far away, anyway.'

His eyes lengthened, and he relinquished his grasp of the pen.

'Thank you. Thank you so much,' Madeleine uttered, adjusting herself once more.

'Aren't you going to read what I've written?'

Madeleine giggled nervously, and hurriedly opened the pages to the Travis Yardley biography taking up an entire side of the brochure. She scanned the words but didn't take them in as the warmth of another flush came to her cheeks.

'Thank you,' she said softly.

Travis looked down at his watch. 'Do you, maybe… have time for a drink somewhere, or do you need to—'

'Yes, absolutely,' she said, barely stopping herself from grabbing him. 'That would be…' Her breath ran out before she could end the sentence.

'Great. Where's a good place to go where we can hear ourselves talk?'

'Um, there's a small bar down on Kingsmead Square. We could go there if you like? It's really quite nice. It has beer and wine and everything.'

Travis laughed. 'That sounds perfect. I like beer and wine.' He touched her shoulder. 'And everything.' He raised a brow, and Madeleine tittered nervously.

'You'll have to lead the way; I have no idea where I'm going in this town.'

'Oh, yes,' Madeleine giggled. 'Um, it's this way.'

She began walking away from the theatre towards Monmouth Street, constantly checking over her shoulder that Travis Yardley was *really* coming with her. As they passed couples and groups walking towards them, she wanted to scream out with pride that she was with Travis Yardley, but she also wanted him just to herself. The last thing she needed now was a drunken floozy taking his attention away from her.

A few short moments later, they were entering a dimly-lit wine bar, recently refurbished with tall, leather burgundy-coloured half-moon booths, just perfect for a private tete a tete.

Travis ordered a double rum and coke and a raspberry Bellini for Madeleine. They clinked glasses and said "cheers" in unison.

'What is it?' he asked her after a few moments as Madeleine struggled to make conversation.

'No one would believe me. No one would believe *this*.'

'Why not?'

'Because…'

Travis dipped his head provocatively.

'Oh, come on. You're gorgeous. And famous. And gorgeous, and you're in here with me.'

'Yes, I am… here with you.'

Madeleine giggled again.

His phone rang again, and he waved a dismissive hand as it rang off after the twentieth ring.

'So,' he said, looking around at the other booths. 'What brings you out tonight… alone?'

'I love the theatre. You just cannot beat the intensity of a live performance.'

'I agree. There's nothing more invigorating than feeling the passion and emotion.'

They shared a smile.

'Can I ask?' she said. 'Do you mind playing a baddie?'

Travis smiled with his lengthening eyes and took a long sip from his drink as he held her stare. 'Do you like bad boys?'

Madeleine hooked fallen hair away from her face. 'Well, I like your bad boy,' she blushed.

'Good.'

'Um, do you mind me commenting on something?'

'Be my guest.'

'I thought you were from London?'

Travis brought his glass towards his lips, and he licked the rim of the glass with the tip of his tongue before he took another gulp. 'Are you going to answer my question?' he asked.

Madeleine rubbed the side of her neck. 'Which question?'

'Why are you out alone?'

'I… I didn't have anyone to come with.'

His eyes narrowed. 'You live by yourself?'

'Yes…' she said hesitantly. 'Well, kind of.' She rubbed the side of her neck and looked away.

'Kind of…?'

'I look after my mother. She's got dementia. We live together.'

Travis turned his face.

'She lives in the main house,' Madeleine quickly qualified. 'I live in the annexe… by myself.'

'I see.'

He stared at her intently with his dark chocolaty eyes. 'If you don't mind me saying?'

She nodded eagerly.

'I thought you were a little too old to be still living with Mum and Dad.'

'I'm twenty-nine, I'll have you know,' Madeleine bit playfully.

'And incredibly beautiful with it.'

Madeleine looked down at the table and felt the flush of embarrassment once more.

'How about you?' she braced herself to ask. 'Do you live with anyone?'

'Me? No. I'm always… transient.'

'I read… um, sorry,' she giggled anxiously, 'um, what if the right person came along?'

Travis leaned back in the seat and looked left and right. The booths were completely private, apart from the staff collecting or delivering glasses.

He lunged forwards and grasped the sides of Madeleine's head, gently coaxing her face towards his waiting lips. She didn't resist, and soon, they were enjoying a long, passionate kiss.

'Maybe you just have,' he said as their faces parted.

'Do you want to come back to my hotel?' he asked. 'It's quite beautiful.'

'Yes… no, oh, ah…I can't. I have to get home for Mum.'

Madeleine now appreciated how it must feel to lose a winning lottery ticket.

Travis dipped his head and looked at her from beneath his sultry lids.

'Okay, how far away is home?'

'Twenty minutes in a taxi… what?' she said as the implication of what he was asking hit her like a double-decker bus. 'You really want to come back to my house?'

'Yes, I do. Really.'

'Oh my God!'

Madeleine bit the inside of her lip as she considered what Travis Yardley was putting on a plate – her plate. He *actually* wanted to go home with her. Did he mean to sleep with her? That's how it was coming across. She wouldn't object, my God! *I mean, how stupid would that be?*

The thoughts and questions raced around her floating head. Her mother would be asleep, and she had no neighbours to speak of, not for several hundred metres, anyway.

'Okay,' she said breathlessly.

'Good. Let's have another drink. Do you like champagne?'

Madeleine let out a stifled giggle. 'Yes,' she spluttered.

They did their best to enter the modern barn conversion on the edge of Hinton Charterhouse with the dexterity of a surgeon; however, neither of them succeeded, and they both spilt in through the door to giggles of "*Shhhhh*".

No sooner had the door closed than Travis had Madeleine pinned up against the side of the hallway wall, their lips entwined, their hands exploring one another's bodies with the frantic eagerness of young lovers.

'Not here,' Madeleine panted as she fought for her breath.

She took Travis by the hand and led him swiftly through the wide entrance hallway to a beautifully-appointed bedroom with crisp white sheets and a luxurious four-poster bed taking centre stage of the warm stone-clad room. Soft lighting caught the shimmer of delicate lace draped on either side of the bed.

'Perfect,' Travis commented in a low voice.

Madeleine walked him to the edge of the bed, sat down in front of him and hastily unbuttoned his shirt, quickly followed by the buckle of his jeans.

His clothes fell to the floor around his feet, and he grabbed Madeleine by the shoulders and encouraged her backwards onto the bed, straddling her prone body.

He kissed her mouth, neck, and earlobes and slowly moved down towards her chest, opening the buttons of her blouse with the gentleness of two people exploring one another for the first time.

He stopped shy of her breasts. 'I have an idea,' he said, inches from her skin.

'Yes,' Madeleine said, her body writhing with delight.

'You said you had always wanted to be an actress.'

'Yes.'

'Does *this* remind you of anything?'

Her eyes opened, and she stared at the wooden frame of the four-poster bed. 'The murder scene from the show?'

Travis let out a puff of air against her heaving bosom.

'You know, I don't actually rate Holly Delgado.' He raised himself to look at Madeleine. 'I've often wondered how much better it would be with someone different.'

He pushed his hands into the soft duvet on either side of Madeleine's head.

'Why don't you try?'

Madeleine giggled. 'But it doesn't end well for Gemma in the show.'

Travis sat up and leaned his weight back through his bottom, pinning Madeleine's legs to the bed.

He opened his mouth and tracked his eyes over her body.

'Now, something's missing?'

'Um, the knife… can't we just imagine that bit?'

'No, we cannot.'

He sprang from the bed and rushed out of the room.

Madeleine scratched beneath her ear, re-buttoned the bottom of her blouse and pulled her legs up into a sitting position, and hugged her knees.

As she waited for Travis to return, she did her best to sober up by attempting to focus on the small digital alarm clock on the bedside dresser.

12:17, or is it 12:11?

Looking over towards the door, she saw the shadow of Travis approaching silently in the semi-darkness.

'Gemma,' he said; his American accent stronger than before. 'You have been a nasty girl.'

'I'm Madeleine. I don't like this. Please stop.'

He grabbed her ankles and pulled her feet towards him.

Before she could respond, he was straddling her body, this time pinning her to the bed with the force of his thighs.

'Travis, I don't like this,' Madeleine whimpered.

'Shut up, bitch,' he said, slapping her face with ferocity. 'You've done me wrong, and now you must pay.'

He grabbed her throat and squeezed so hard that Madeleine could barely breathe.

'You have wronged me for the last time, Gemma.'

He released his grasp and raised both hands high above his head.

As Madeleine struggled to re-gain her breath, she caught the glint of steel between his balled fists. Instinctively, she tried to squirm away but his body weight fixed to the spot.

What are the fucking lines? She struggled to remember as pure fear gushed through her veins.

'No, Jesse…' she said, remembering the scene from the show. 'I–I promise—'

Travis smiled menacingly. 'It's too late for promises, bitch.'

He thrust the blade down with all the force he could muster.

CHAPTER ONE

Sunday 6th March

3:51 a.m.

'Yes,' Detective Inspector Robbie Chilcott answered, forcing his gummy eyes apart. 'DI Chilcott.'

'Hello, sir,' a hesitant female voice replied. 'Apologies for the lateness of the call.'

Chilcott's blinking eyes cut through the blackness of the bedroom and fixed on the green LED alarm clock display on a table opposite him.

Bloody hell, what now?

'Yes,' he said. 'Who am I talking with?'

'Acting Inspector, Chloe Spencer, sir. I'm the night tour supervisor at Echo Bravo.'

'Bath, eh? What's going on in sleepy old Bath that warrants me being woken up at this ungodly hour?'

'As I say, I'm really sorry to bother you with this, sir. But you are shown as being the on-call DI, is that correct?'

'Yes, I am. Unfortunately. Go on; you'd better tell me what's happening?'

'We have a chap at the Royal United Hospital. He was brought in by ambulance an hour ago. Basically, he was covered head to toe in what appears to be blood. However, a full-body examination has shown that he has no visible signs of injury.'

'And?'

'The accident and emergency sister called us because if it's not his blood, then it belongs to someone or something else, sir.'

Chilcott brought himself up to a seated position, propped a pillow behind the small of his back and leaned his head back against the headboard.

'So, exactly how much blood are we talking about here?'

'I'm looking at a bin liner full to the brim with blood-soaked swabs and towels, sir.'

Chilcott pressed the speakerphone tab, dropped the phone to his lap, rubbed his eyes with the bony second joint of each index finger and yawned widely.

'Okay, now you've got me up, you may as well tell me about the circumstances – briefly – I don't need to know the ins and outs of a dog's arse, okay?'

'Of course, sir. The man was located near Hinton Charterhouse on the B3110 in the direction of Bath shortly after two o'clock this morning. He was found wearing only underpants at the time. Believing a bad accident had occurred somewhere, a passing taxi driver called it in on the nines. An ambulance was dispatched, located the male further along the road and brought him to accident and emergency.'

'But he wasn't injured?'

'It appears not, sir. The ambulance crew did call for police attendance at the time, but there was no one available to meet them at the roadside, so they brought him in for a more detailed assessment.'

'Has that section of road been checked for RTCs?'

'There are no reported road traffic collisions in that area and my team has driven every which route from Hinton Charterhouse and can find no evidence of a single-vehicle crash either on or off the road, sir.'

'Who is he, this bloke?'

'We've been given a name from the hospital staff, but he's coming up no trace on the police national computer. He isn't providing any information to help us contact his next of kin, etcetera. And he obviously didn't have any identification on him due to his state of undress at the time he was located.'

'What name have you been given?'

'Jesse Garcia, sir.'

'That's not a name on my radar.'

'He sounds American from his accent, sir.'

'Is he living in the Hinton Charterhouse area? Do we know that much?'

'We don't know much about him at all, I'm afraid, sir. He's not really giving us straight answers, and we are being careful not to ask anything that would constitute an interview.'

'Just make sure you document everything you ask him and everything he replies.'

'Well, that's not much, to be honest, sir. He's very difficult to talk to. That was one reason why the paramedics brought him to accident and emergency so that he could have a full assessment.'

'Are we thinking about a head injury here?'

'Possibly. The man had blood inside his mouth. The hospital is keeping him under observation, at least until the doctors have a chance to see him in the morning.'

'So, what do you need from me right now?' Chilcott rolled his head towards the clock. 'At three fifty-four in the morning?'

Acting Inspector Spencer hesitated. 'Um… it was just to make you aware that this had come in and to check there was nothing more that we should be considering at this moment in time, sir?'

'Such as?'

'He was completely covered in blood, sir.'

Chilcott rubbed his forehead and stifled a groan away from the mouthpiece. 'You say there's bin bag full of swabs. It won't do any harm to seize them along with his underwear. Secure them in the appropriate forensic packaging and book them into the detained property. That way, we won't lose out if he turns out to be a crazed psycho killer.'

The line was silent for a few seconds.

'Is there something else?' Chilcott asked reluctantly.

'What if there's a body somewhere, sir?'

Chilcott massaged his brow with his fingertips as the bleak prospect of such a scenario played out in his mind.

'If there's a body somewhere, Mr Garcia has some talking to do. I'm on call again tomorrow – I mean today, but I'm going into the office for a bit for my sins. Do what you can for now. Secure the swabs and find out which nurses cleaned him up, just in case we need statements from them at a later date. Let's see what his condition is in the morning, whether he'll be staying at the hospital for any length of time, and then we'll take it from there.'

Chilcott ended the call and fell back to sleep with relative ease within two minutes.

CHAPTER TWO

The alarm woke him at seven. He dressed in his suit, shirt and tie, sank a couple of coffees and swiftly devoured two bagels smeared with lemon curd. That was one habit his first wife used to despise; she hated lemon curd with a passion. That only made Chilcott want to eat it more, and now he was practically dependent on the stuff.

It was unusual for Chilcott to be working on a Sunday without a specific case to progress, but he was doing a favour for a friend who should have been covering the duty DI gig that weekend. And being a prisoner to the "DI hotline" since Saturday lunchtime, he figured he might as well be in the office clearing some admin, which was never one of his more accomplished tasks.

His desk phone rang, and he picked it up on the third ring.

'DI Chilcott.'

'Robbie, it's Davie.'

Chilcott recognised the voice of his occasional golfing opponent, Bath CID Detective Sergeant David Andrews.

Davie was playing off a nine handicap – Chilcott in the high teens. They shared a dark sense of humour, a liking for Bath Ales and had roughly the same win/loss ratio thanks to Chilcott's inflated handicap.

'Davie, what's happening, you old bugger? Are you calling to give me a chance to win my twenty back?'

'Wish I was, mate. We'll sort something out soon. Maybe head up to Lansdown for a round. Just make sure you bring your A-game. I'm pretty consistent at the moment.'

'Yeah, yeah, I've heard all that before. Anyway, what can I do for you, mate?'

'I heard you were going to be in the office today, which is why I didn't call your mobile. This overnight job in Bath; the American—'

'Yeah, I know about that. Some acting inspector called me in the middle of the night.'

'That's right. There's something not right about this job, Robbie.'

Chilcott pulled his daybook closer to him and scribbled the date at the top of a blank page.

'All right. Has your team picked up the investigation?'

'Yes, and I know it's early days, but I think we need to raise the flag.'

Chilcott groaned to himself. That was news he didn't want to hear.

'Okay, Davie. Hit me with it…'

'The male has been assessed in A&E and has now been referred to a psychiatric outpatient ward for their opinion.'

'That sounds about right. The officer told me last night that the male appeared confused.'

'I don't like it,' Davie said. 'He is covered in blood – at

least that's what it looks like. And it's not his own. He was discovered in the middle of nowhere. He is only in his undercrackers, and is unable or unwilling to provide us with any concrete information about who he is or where he's from.'

'What does the hospital say about his condition?'

'They are wondering if he's experienced a recent trauma of some kind, leading to his confused and vacant presentation.'

'Like what?'

'Who knows? I've seen the number of swabs used to clean him up, and if it turns out to be blood, we're not talking about a nicked finger here.'

'Has anyone been back to the location where he was discovered in daylight hours?'

'Uniformed officers have been out and taken a good look around. I'm satisfied that there is nothing obvious for us to find at the roadside.'

'That's Midford Valley if I'm not mistaken?'

'That's right.'

'Steep embankments down one side?'

'Yep.'

'Have you guys got a drone operator at the station to take a look down over the edge?'

'We've checked the route and hedgerows on both sides. I'm confident there are no cars down the side of the valley.'

Chilcott placed the phone on the loudspeaker, leaned back in his seat and cupped the back of his head with his hands. 'Well then, I think it's time we check the hospital swabs for DNA,' he said.

'A wise and valid line of enquiry, given his lack of injuries, Robbie.'

'Okay. Let's see if this male will give us an elimination DNA sample while we've got him at the hospital. If we can identify the blood-like substance to be from an innocent source, then we can dispose of the samples before we go to any more expense with them.'

'From what I've heard, I can't think what possible innocent source that would be unless he's a midwife who delivers babies in his underwear.'

'Hold up – you might not be too far off the mark with that. What if that is the scenario? His partner has given birth at home, and he's helped deliver the baby. It would account for his state of undress being the small hours of the morning, and it would also account for any large quantities of blood found on him. It might even justify his dazed demeanour – I remember my shock at seeing the amount of claret when my daughter was born. I reckon there would have been less blood at an abattoir. Do we have officers with him now?'

'Yes, I tasked a couple of my team to head up to the hospital and check out the situation. I'll put in a request for CSI to examine the swabs.'

'Let's do that sooner rather than later. Any problems, tell them I authorised it.'

'Don't worry; I'll get on it.'

'I hate to bother her before we have more information, but I'll give the DCI a call and give her a heads-up of the job.'

'Thanks, Rob. I'm really sorry to have bothered you with this, and I'm sure it will be something of nothing.'

'No worries. It's better to be safe than sorry. Just imagine the fallout if it turns out this bloke has butchered someone, and we've turned a blind eye.'

CHAPTER THREE

Chilcott spent the next two hours wading through his admin tasks. He had half a mind on the hospital case and the other half thinking about Bette Reynard, a Special Branch operative working in Paris. He had the unexpected pleasure of meeting her back in August when he was investigating the disappearance of a woman from a luxury yacht. They instantly clicked. She was about his age, single, wildly attractive, with an asymmetrical bobbed hairstyle that accentuated her chic good looks. In fact, she was everything Chilcott was not, but she seemed to enjoy his company as much as he did hers. He had kept it quiet from the others, but Bette was coming to the UK at the end of the week for work-related matters and was staying in London for six nights. Amazingly, she had contacted him about the visit and asked if he had any time off to meet up, which was how he came to be covering the DI duties over this weekend. Because the plan was to travel up to London on Friday after work, stay for the weekend in cheap accommodation and travel back on Sunday night. At least, that was the plan. Chilcott couldn't help but sense the hospital job would put his romantic liaison to the test.

He checked his watch. 11:47 a.m. With no update from Bath, he dug out his phone and called DS Andrews.

'Davie, it's Robbie. What's the update on our John Doe?'

'I'm still at the hospital. CSI officers have taken the swabs away with them, and I'm waiting for an update. We have a little problem, though; they want to discharge Garcia as he no longer poses a medical concern.'

'Has he provided them with a discharge address?'

'Speaking to the ward sister, it transpires that the only address Garcia will provide them is a Fort Lauderdale address in Florida. He's not providing a fixed place of abode in the UK.'

'That's not very helpful.'

'The medical team say he is physically fit for discharge, and they are keen to free up his bed. Reading between the lines, I think our interest in him has provided them with the opportunity to leave any worries about his domestic arrangements in our court.'

The end of a plastic Bic biro repeatedly tapped against the side of Chilcott's temple with a fast metronomic uniformity as he pondered the next move.

Suddenly, the tapping stopped. 'Let's bring him in for a voluntary interview,' Chilcott said. 'He's certainly got some questions to answer, and that may gift us a few more hours to establish who and what we are dealing with here?'

'What if he refuses to come with us?'

'Don't give him the option. I'm sure you can use your powers of persuasion.'

'Noted.'

'How does he seem today?'

Andrews emitted a soft sigh. 'Ah… he appears pretty relaxed about the whole thing. If I didn't know better, I'd say he was enjoying the attention.'

'Hmmm. Is he offering any more information that we didn't already know?'

'Nothing. He speaks when spoken to, but not with any depth. He isn't what I'd call a chatty person.'

'Has anyone approached the hospital inquiring about him, do you know?'

'That was one of the first things I checked when we arrived. They've had no phone calls and no one asking after him.'

'Do you think that's odd?'

'I do, yes. Imagine if you were brought in – no, scrub that, no one would come for you either—'

'Cheeky sod,' Chilcott chuckled.

'In all seriousness, it's reasonable to imagine someone somewhere might be concerned about him?'

'Okay,' Chilcott said, rising from his seat. 'I'll inform Keynsham Police Custody Centre that'll you'll be coming over soon. Although this is a voluntary interview, my gut feeling says we should use a video interview room. Just in case.'

'Fine by me. We should be there within the hour. The hospital seems keen as mustard to kick him out.'

'Okay, let me know when you arrive at custody. I'd quite like to see what the cause for my disrupted sleep looks like with my own eyes. I'll also contact CSI in the meantime and make sure they expedite the results from the swabs.'

· · ·

Chilcott searched through the phone list and found the number for the CSI department at Falcon Road Police Station, Bath. Soon, he was talking to duty CSI officer Melanie Sellars.

'I'm chasing up the results of the swabs taken from the hospital. I need to know if we are looking at human blood?'

'I'm afraid I can't tell you that at this time, sir,' CSI Sellars said.

'Well, what can you tell me?'

'We ran a presumptive test for the presence of haemoglobin – it's called a Kastle-Meyer test, sir.'

'Yes, yes, and what did that prove?'

'It doesn't prove anything, sir. But it was a positive test, suggesting the substance recovered was haemoglobin-based blood.'

'So, it could be from a human, a cow, a horse, a dog, or even a rat?'

'Unlikely to be a rat, sir.'

'I was being flippant.'

Chilcott rubbed a hand down his face. 'So, what can you tell me about this blood?'

'The Kastle-Meyer test only provides us with the confirmation that we are looking at blood, sir. We would need to send the samples off to the laboratory for further testing to establish if we are looking at human blood.'

'How long will that take?'

'A standard submission will usually return within seven to ten days. An urgent submission should be back within forty-eight hours, sir.'

'We don't have forty-eight hours, let alone ten days. Is there any way we can get the results sooner?'

'I'm afraid not, sir. And as it stands, no one has autho-rised the submission for further analysis.'

'Consider it authorised – put my name against the request. Make sure it's marked as urgent.'

'It'll cost more to obtain an urgent result, sir. I just need to make you aware of that.'

'Don't worry about costs. Where does the sample get sent?'

'To our lab in Chepstow.'

'How does it get there?'

'Once the order is requested, a courier will come and transport it to the lab.'

'How long will that take?'

'Samples are normally collected within six hours, sir.'

'Jesus,' Chilcott spluttered. 'I'll drive the bloody sample there myself. It'll be a darn sight quicker.'

'That has been known, sir.'

Chilcott drifted off into his thoughts. Was he being too hasty? Was he jumping to pessimistic conclusions? He had been in the job a long time, and he knew his take on life was tainted by the many horrors he'd encountered over decades of dealing with the dregs and pond-life of society.

'We still don't know if we have a victim somewhere?' Chilcott muttered in answer to his questioning mind.

'I'm sorry, sir?' CSI Sellars said.

'Oh, nothing, look… if I can find a willing volunteer to drive the samples up to the lab right away, what are the chances of getting the results within the next twenty-four hours or, at worst, by the end of play tomorrow?'

'I obviously can't make any guarantees, sir, because I can't speak on behalf of the lab. But you'll stand a much better chance than if we use the normal method of delivery.'

'Good. Make sure the sample is good to go. I'll find a traffic unit to take the sample up to Chepstow. I've yet to find a traffic officer who doesn't love screaming up the motorway like their pants are on fire.'

CHAPTER FOUR

Keynsham Police Centre was a generic design of the modern era with little to distinguish it as a hive for police officers. If anything, it looked more like a call centre, or a sofa outlet, or a trading estate supermarket. Minus the trays of dried-out, decaying potted plants or pallets stacked high with bags of potting soil and charcoal. Perhaps the only giveaway to the uninitiated eye was the high wire fence that kept staff cars at a secure arm's length from any disgruntled shits who might be passing on their way back home from a night in the cells. Of course, the Avon and Somerset Police Constabulary crest emblazoned on one corner of the frontage. It wasn't that Chilcott disliked the new-builds or their locations, nor even the ever-clunking cogs of change. No – it was the flat-packed simplistic lack of character of it all. The overwhelming blandness. The overriding sense of… well, meh! There had been nothing wrong with the likes of Trinity Road or Staple Hill, except perhaps they were costing the force a small fortune. Even his beloved old station at Wells was now a development of luxury flats. And as he romanticised about the good old days, he watched as two young uniformed officers walked uninterestedly towards a marked police unit, and it struck him; it wasn't just the buildings now that lacked character.

Located between Bath and the south-eastern edge of Bristol, the Keynsham nick was now one of only three super-custody units in the entire force area. Arrested suspects were brought here from far and wide for stacking, grilling and dispatching. Most got to leave under the steam of their own two feet. However, a small percentage of others left the building in the back of a meat wagon with a one-way ticket to a remand centre and the prospect of a court deciding their foreseeable destiny. For Chilcott, that was half of the fun; finding the real bad'uns and getting the bastards off the streets.

'I thought you said you'd be about an hour?' Chilcott barked as the district CID detectives strode in through the main entrance door and directed the mysterious American to take a seat in one of the bolted-down soft seats against the wall. He was dressed in standard custody unit apparel, normally given to suspects who have had their own clothes seized for forensic purposes, or because they have spoiled. Chilcott gave his subject a serious once-over.

'I've been waiting here getting on for two hours,' Chilcott said. He hadn't. He just wanted to emphasise the point that he had been made to wait for longer than he would have liked.

'Sorry, sir,' one of the district detectives said. 'There were problems with the mental health discharge team at the hospital.'

Chilcott beckoned the officer towards him with a

twitching finger and took the officer to the opposite side of the room where they wouldn't be overheard.

'Problems? What sort of problems?' Chilcott asked. 'Does this individual have mental health issues?'

'Apparently not, sir,' the detective replied with more than an accent of surprise in his tone. 'Without any history of mental health and with the odd, yet unconcerning behaviour displayed, they said their hands were effectively tied.'

'I need to know we've covered all bases before we interview this character.'

The officer nodded. 'Yes, sir.'

'So, are we happy he doesn't need an appropriate adult with him during the interview?'

'Absolutely certain, sir. I asked the discharging doctor that exact same question. He said it was down to us, but he could see no medical reason why he would need additional assistance during an interview.'

'That'll do me,' Chilcott said, glancing back towards the seated American, who was staring forwards into space with an oddly serene smile.

'The room is set up and good to go,' Chilcott said. 'I reserved the video interview room. Take him through, and I'll watch proceedings from the satellite room. I'm dying to hear just what he has to say about all that blood.'

The satellite room was just a few doors away. A compact and cluttered box room filled with sealed packs of freeze-dried coffee and other consumables. Chilcott had a 46-inch front-row seat to the ongoing interrogation of the mysterious, and as yet, unflappable American. A small CCTV camera pitched above the interview room door was beaming live footage to Chilcott's wall-mounted monitor. Chilcott wasn't taking any chances, and he'd set the equipment to record the interview – just in case.

Although Jesse Garcia was not under arrest, he still had the opportunity to be represented by a solicitor, and Chilcott was inwardly delighted when Garcia declined that particular privilege. Yet, as he watched on, Chilcott's trained and experienced eye couldn't help but notice how relaxed and at ease Garcia appeared, confronted by the two detectives seated opposite him.

'This interview is being audibly and visually recorded. You are not under arrest, and you are free to leave at any time,' the main interviewing detective said.

Chilcott leaned towards the screen and watched for a reaction.

'You are entitled to free and independent legal advice, which includes the right to speak to a solicitor on the telephone. You have so far declined legal advice. Are you happy to continue this interview without first speaking with a lawyer?'

'I am,' Garcia responded simply.

'Fine. I need to caution you before we ask you any questions. You do not have to say anything. But it may harm your defence if you do not mention when questioned something which you later rely on in court. And anything you do say may be given in evidence. Is that understood?'

Garcia smiled.

The first officer looked sideways at his colleague, who bobbed his head for the interview to begin in earnest.

'Tell me about yourself,' the first detective said.

'Wodda you wonna know?' Garcia answered with a soft Southern-American vernacular.

'Let's begin with who you are?'

'Jesse Garcia.' He smiled broadly at the second detective who jotted the answer into his daybook.

'And what is your date of birth, please, Mr Garcia?'

'February-eighth. Seventy-three.'

'Making you…'

I am forty-eight years of age.'

The second officer peered back at Garcia over the top of his specs for a long moment before circling the age in his daybook.

'Where do you live?' the first officer asked.

Garcia blinked once and then turned his face away and sighed loudly.

'Mr Garcia. Your address?'

'I live in the Tampa Heights district of Florida.'

'Okay.'

The second officer noted the location.

'So, what are you doing in the UK?'

Garcia smiled, hooked his hands behind his head and rocked back on the rear legs of his plastic seat. Being a voluntary interview, they were not in the custody unit. As a result, the decor in the room wasn't bolted to the floor, unlike *through the doors*.

'I'm kicking back. Taking in the scenery. Eating fish and chips,' he said with a feeble attempt at a London Cockney accent. His white teeth beamed back at the officers like a row of stubby glow sticks at a teeny-bopper concert.

'I'm not concerned with your eating habits while you're here, Mr Garcia,' the DC came back.

'Suit yourself,' he grinned and brought his chair back down onto four legs.

'But I am concerned with where you have been staying while you are in the UK?'

'Ah, you know. Here and there. There and here.'

'Mr Garcia. Just let me explain how this works a little clearer. Perhaps the concept of this interview wasn't explained in enough detail by me at the start. I'm sorry.'

Garcia held up his palms. 'Hey, no problem, man.'

The detective gave his subject a fixed stare.

'When I ask you a question, I expect a detailed answer,' he said. '"Here and there, there and here", well, that *is not* a detailed answer.'

The officer paused, taking a breath.

'So, please… where are you staying in the UK right now?'

Garcia looked between the two officers in turn and then chuckled. 'Come on… I'm with you guys.'

The first detective's voice tightened, his impatience becoming increasingly apparent.

'You were picked up from the roadside in the early hours of this morning near Hinton Charterhouse. What address had you come from, or what address were you going towards?'

Garcia's grin gradually faded, and he leaned forwards and interlocked his fingers together on the desktop before slowly withdrawing them and lowering them into his lap. His once smiling eyes had now narrowed to unfriendly heavy lids, and he shrugged his shoulders to the question.

'If you don't mind me saying,' the second detective said, 'you are now coming across as defensive and evasive. That could make us question the reason why?'

Garcia looked around the four corners of the room before settling his eyes on the red-dotted camera facing him.

'Wouldn't you be?' he said, turning back to the second detective.

'I guess that depends.'

Garcia stared at the second detective for an uncompromising ten or more seconds.

'On what?' he finally said.

'If I'd been discovered walking down a country road in my boxer shorts in the middle of the night and covered from head to foot in blood, I'd probably feel a bit arse-twitchy right now too.'

A smile curled upward on one side of Garcia's lips.

'What's so amusing?' the first detective asked.

Garcia's whimsical smile quickly turned into a confident smirk.

'You guys,' he said, leaning back again, using a rigid index finger to point between the officers. 'Is it true most British cops don't carry guns?'

'That's probably correct,' the first detective said, leaning his body towards Garcia. 'But gun or no gun, we're no less effective.'

Garcia laughed and raised a thumb behind his pointed finger and brought it towards his line of sight. He held it for five seconds on each officer as if it were a gun. His aim settled on the first detective, and he lowered his thumb with a click of his cheek and then blew imaginary smoke from the tip of his index finger.

'Thankfully, British cops are also immune to finger guns, Mr Garcia,' the first detective said, unimpressed by his subject's bravado. 'Now, back to the interview. Where's your passport?'

'I dunno?' Garcia shrugged.

'Do you know it is an offence not to be in possession of your passport upon the request of an official when on foreign soils, Mr Garcia?'

'I do now,' he beamed.

'So, where is it?'

He shrugged the question away with a pout. 'Like I said…'

'When did you come into the country?'

'Do you know what… I can't exactly recall?'

'Do you have the slightest inclination of how serious this interview could be for your current liberty, Mr Garcia?'

'Do you think I'm an illegal? Is that what this is? *Pfft,*' he puffed through his lips.

'All right,' the first detective said, pressing both palms down onto the tabletop. 'There are two ways we can do this. You either comply with these very simple questions, or we can do this the hard way. I don't mind. I'm getting paid either way.' He stared at Garcia. 'Do you understand what I'm telling you?'

'Ummm?' Garcia mused with a finger to his lips.

'You were picked up in the middle of nowhere. Wearing only boxer shorts and you were covered in blood. I think it's about time you told us everything you know about that.'

Garcia cupped a hand and rested his chin inside it, blinking slowly as he looked at the two detectives. He then cocked his head towards the closed door.

'Don't even think about it,' Detective one said. 'Mr Garcia, at the moment, you are here voluntarily, and we have shown you courtesy and patience. In theory, that means you can leave this interview at any time. But let me tell you this. If you don't start giving satisfactory answers to all of our questions, we will be forced to arrest you and keep you detained in one of our cells until we can satisfy ourselves that you are innocent of any ill-doing.'

Garcia's mood flashed to anger. 'Arrest me? For what? Taking a walk in my shorts?'

'The blood smeared over your body is currently being analysed by forensic officers,' the first detective said. 'Unless you can provide us with a reasonable explanation of how that blood came to be on your person, we will have no alternative but to arrest you for securing and preserving evidence while we conduct a prompt and effective investigation.'

Garcia pulled his arms in tightly to his side and hunched forwards. He was going into protective mode.

Chilcott jumped up from his viewing seat and made directly for the interview room.

He banged loudly three times and waited for the door to open.

The second officer's face appeared in the gap of the door.

'Pause the interview,' Chilcott said. 'I need one of you out here with me, please.'

The second detective went back inside for a brief moment and returned to Chilcott in the corridor.

'So, let's just look at what we have here,' Chilcott said to the officer. 'We've got an American who won't or can't give us full details of who he is, or where he's from. Or what he's doing walking down the middle of a country road at night, wearing his kecks and covered in someone or something else's blood. Am I correct in thinking that's about the size of it?'

'Yes, sir,' the detective answered.

'Alright. Now let's think about what we don't have?'

'We don't have a crime. We don't have a victim,' the officer said.

Chilcott pointed at him. 'We don't have a victim. And, we don't have a crime scene.'

The detective nodded.

'We might not have either of these things, but I've seen enough blood in my career to know that we can't turn a blind eye to this. So, here's what we do,' Chilcott said, 'we can't let him go – so arrest him on suspicion of murder. He can stew for a few hours in a cell, and we buy ourselves some time to dig a little deeper. Let's swamp the area with officers where he was found. Get another dog down there and see if we can track where he came from. I know we've lost valuable time, but we need to try everything here. If the blood comes back as animal DNA, we're looking at a different kind of nutter, and we need to consider our options. If the blood comes back as human DNA, then we're in trouble. And in that scenario, we are up against the clock, and we need to find the source of that blood pretty damn quick.'

'Sir?' the detective interrupted.

'Yes.'

The officer had a tight face. 'I've never dealt with anything like this before.'

Chilcott placed a hand on the detective's shoulder. 'It's

an odd one for sure, son. So, let's all pray this turns out to be something of nothing.'

'What should we do if Garcia continues to say nothing, sir?'

'I don't think we'll get anything more from him today – we haven't got anything on him. You can't blame him for not talking. So, we'll do what we always do, son. We turn over every stone. We secure each tiny strand of evidence. And we hope.'

'Hope for what, sir?'

Chilcott turned away.

'Sir?'

Chilcott snapped. 'We hope we're not too late.' He looked at his watch. 'Nearly four-twenty,' he said. 'Right, get back in there. Arrest that bastard on suspicion of murder, and let's get him locked up.'

CHAPTER FIVE

Monday 7th March

8:17 a.m.

The Bristol Central Major Crime Investigation Team had been in the briefing room for just over fifteen minutes. An overnight stabbing had been allocated to a team of six eager-looking detectives. The twenty-seven-year-old victim was reported to be in a serious yet stable condition in the ITU section of the Bristol Royal Infirmary. He was under armed police protection. He was suspected of being a lead player in one of Bristol's most active and well-organised street gangs. His attack would most likely escalate tensions between rival criminal fraternities and the powers that be expected revenge justice.

Fresh from the success of a recent fraud case, DC Richie Allen would be the Officer in the Case as he continued to grow his impressive portfolio of criminal investigations. Chilcott's equal, Detective Inspector Jasjit Chowdhury would oversee the stabbing investigation, which would likely be a long, drawn-out case due to the unsupportive nature of those involved. Thanks to the four separate and self-contained incident rooms, the major crime team could facilitate several simultaneous inquiries. All they needed was staff to fill them, which was the challenge.

Before Chowdhury and his team escaped to their duties, DCI Julie Foster addressed the room.

'Just to make you all aware and put you on notice, we have a second job that came in during the early hours of yesterday morning near Bath. It's a bit of an odd one, and at this present moment, we have no evidence to confirm that a criminal offence has taken place. However, the unusual circumstances are such that we would be prudent to keep a very close eye on proceedings. DI Chilcott was on cover duties at the weekend and made the call to go in at the high-end and arrest the suspect on suspicion of murder.'

The DCI stopped talking, noticing several pairs of eyes rolling from the team working on the street gang stabbing.

'Don't fret. Don't fret,' DCI Foster said. 'Bath CID are picking up the case in the first instance. But I've promised them DI Chilcott for a day or two, just to oversee the early stages of the investigation in a purely supervisory capacity. We hope this job won't trouble us in the long run, and I know DI Chilcott will do all he can to keep the job with the district boys and girls.'

A sideways glance towards her DI was more an instruction than a statement.

The DCI paused and looked around the room. 'I'm

looking for a detective to assist DI Chilcott at short notice, should the need arise.'

DC McEwan raised his hand.

'Sean, thank you. Tie up with Inspector Chilcott, and he'll brief you with the job details.'

Chilcott looked across the briefing room at DI Chowdhury, who was *sitting pretty*, so to speak. He didn't resent Chowdhury having the sexier of the two jobs. Chilcott's prints were already on the John Doe case, so it made sense that he continued overseeing the investigation. Not only that, it was about time Chowdhury had a spell in the limelight. Chilcott had enormous misgivings about Jaz Chowdhury when he first joined the department. Still, Chilcott was happy to be proven wrong over the months of seeing how Chowdhury investigated his caseload and the way he took control of the team. Jaz Chowdhury was an intelligent and hard-working DI, and despite his rapid rise to a position of senior rank as a result of his degree qualifications, Chilcott was pleased he was finally getting his own juicy cases.

Chilcott followed DCI Foster into her office and closed the door firmly behind him.

'Robbie. Something on your mind?'

Chilcott remained beside the closed door, his bottom pressed tightly against it.

'This Hinton case is bothering me,' he said. 'I think we need to put more resources into it.'

'Not until we have a victim,' Foster said bluntly, taking her seat and tapping life back into her computer screen.

'We don't know anything about the bloody victim.'

Foster dipped her head and stared at Chilcott over the top of her reading glasses. 'Exactly.'

'We could have a body out there somewhere bleeding to death, or worse.'

Foster blinked. 'And if that was the case, I'm sure someone would have alerted us to the fact by now; someone who hasn't returned home; someone who hasn't turned up to work; someone who has come across a puddle of blood.' She stared at him resolutely. 'But they haven't.'

Chilcott scowled and walked towards his boss. 'How can you be so indifferent about this?'

'I'm not. I'm being practical. It's now nearly thirty hours since your man was taken to hospital, and we haven't heard so much as a peep about a potential victim. I just find that unusual.'

'What… you think I shouldn't have nicked him?'

'I'm not saying that, Robbie. But as things stand, your *suspect* is all you have to go on.'

'And he's playing silly buggers.'

Foster waved her hands dismissively. 'So why should I give up even more of my resources when the district officers are more than capable of investigating this matter at this present moment in time?'

'What if the blood results come back as human?'

'And what if they don't?'

Chilcott stared at Foster indignantly.

'That's clearly a risk you're prepared to gamble.'

Foster pushed her keyboard away from her and swivelled her chair to face him.

'Look, Robbie. We've only got knowledge of this matter because you were doing a mate a favour with the weekend cover. Think about it. Without that, we would be none the wiser, and I'd have two DIs working on the gang war that is about to erupt in the centre of Bristol. Instead, I have just one.'

Chilcott clenched his jaw with recognition.

'You don't think I should have nicked him.'

'It's done,' Foster said, rising to her feet. 'And the chief has been pestering me about it ever bloody since.' She peered at Chilcott for a long moment. 'The sooner those bloods come back, the better.'

'And then what?'

'And then we can leave it for the district DCs to sort out when the DNA comes back as belonging to an animal.'

Foster gave her DI one last lingering look, turned back to her desk and continued working on the computer.

CHAPTER SIX

Dense mist clung like a heavy blanket to the belly of Midford Valley below Chilcott and McEwan as they drove to higher ground and into the bright winter morning sunshine. The verge at the side of the road glistened as light cut through the thick hedgerow and bounced off tiny ice crystals that had frozen in the sub-zero night air. Chilcott loved this time of year. The freshness of it all. The feeling of cold. The sensation of being alive.

Soon they were approaching Hinton Charterhouse and McEwan pulled the car to the side of the road, where Garcia was picked up by the ambulance.

Chilcott stepped out and wrapped his long winter coat around his body. He crunched his way along the frosty grass verge, feeling the coldness penetrating the toes of his leather Oxford brogues.

He saw wide tyre tracks on the opposite verge where he imagined the ambulance pulled off the road to tend to Garcia. He looked around and studied the terrain. There was nothing here. Just a long frosty stretch of nothingness, except highway, hedgerows and fields on either side.

'What do you think, boss?' McEwan asked, coming alongside Chilcott.

Chilcott shook his head and looked in the direction of Hinton Charterhouse, a kilometre or more ahead.

'To have reached this far, he must have been on foot for some time,' he said. 'There's nothing obvious around; no buildings, no nothing.'

McEwan agreed. 'He must have come from somewhere in Hinton Charterhouse, sir.'

'Or from one of those places on the hill coming up from Midford Valley.' Chilcott looked in that direction. 'But that wouldn't add up if he was picked up walking in this direction.'

He paused, blowing clouds of condensation from his breath. 'Where do we begin?'

'I grew up in a small village, boss. There must be a local shop. That's always a good place to start in a small place like this – everyone knows everyone's business.'

Chilcott padded McEwan on the shoulder. 'Good thinking, son. Let's go mingle with the locals.'

Hinton Charterhouse was a small ancient village approximately six miles from the south side of Bath. Dissected by a four-way crossing at its heart, Hinton Charleymouse, as some locals called it, was a 'drive-on-thru' type of place unless you lived there. With a population of only five hundred, most of the properties lined the main roads with some of the most magnificent older properties set back off minor non-arterial routes.

Chilcott parked in the Fox and Hounds Public House car park, and going by the empty spaces, he assumed they wouldn't be causing any issues by leaving the car here for a while. Opposite, on the other side of the narrow main road, a row of old-looking cottages housed a community store in the centre. And just a stone's throw away, another pub, the Golden Fleece, lay invitingly in wait. This was Chilcott's kind of village; two welcoming pubs, a small convenience store and not much else to sully the mind.

They waited for a rush of four cars to pass before crossing the road. A post office sign was screwed to the stonework above the shop entrance.

Chilcott nudged McEwan with his elbow. 'That's good,' he said. 'More chance of CCTV when there's a post office.'

Both men ducked beneath the low plinth of the doorway and stepped down inside the small shop, which housed a menagerie of useful and useless knick-knacks, tinned produce, fresh vegetables, bags of local potatoes, car screen-wash and even boxed inflatable lilos. The shop oozed "localness".

'Good morning,' Chilcott said, looking around for the post office section.

'Morning,' a frail voice came from behind the low countertop. 'What are you after then, my lover?'

A petite old lady, not much taller than the countertop, stood hunched, clutching a steaming mug of something.

'Do you have a post office?' Chilcott asked.

'Not any more, my lover. They took that away. I wasn't making them enough money. Bloody criminal, if you ask me. I've got some stamps here if that's what you're after. What do you need... first, second?'

'I'm not after stamps, but thanks,' Chilcott said, coming back towards the old lady. 'I was actually wondering if you had any CCTV?'

'CCTV?' she replied, slightly amused by the suggestion. 'What would I need with that, then?'

'I'll take that as a no,' Chilcott said, catching McEwan, who was scoping the walls, and returning his verdict with a shake of the head.

'Where are you boys from, then? Not from round 'ere, that's for sure.'

'Very perceptive,' Chilcott chortled.

'Ave 'e come from Bath?'

'No. In fact, we are from Bristol.'

'Bristol?' the old lady said. 'Are you lost?'

Chilcott chuckled. He already liked the old lady. 'No, we're not lost. We know exactly where we are. How long have you been working in this lovely shop for, my dear?'

'Since I was thirteen.'

'Really? Is that allowed?'

'It's been in my family for three generations.'

'And do you mind me asking your name?' Chilcott said.

'Gladys Small,' the lady answered.

'Pleased to meet you, Gladys,' Chilcott said, giving her hand a gentle shake. 'So, I guess you know pretty much everyone in the village, do you?'

'Mostly.' She looked away. 'I don't much want to know that lot from the new estate, though,' she said with a disapproving tone.

'There's a new estate? I must have missed that as we drove through.'

'How can you miss it? It's a bloody disgrace.'

'Do you mean the estate back in the direction of Bath?'

The old lady nodded and screwed up her wrinkly face.

'They were built back in the early nineties, weren't they?' McEwan chipped in.

'Bloody disgrace,' Gladys Small repeated beneath her breath.

Chilcott gave McEwan a twitch of the brow and a restrained smile.

'I couldn't agree more, Gladys,' Chilcott said. 'Why ruin a beautiful village like this with new-builds. Anyway,' he said, noticing Gladys becoming agitated in her own thoughts. 'We are actually from the police, and we are here because a man was picked up on the main road a couple of nights ago, and we are trying to find out who he is?'

'The police?' Gladys said, looking at Chilcott and McEwan with renewed interest. 'You don't look like police.'

Chilcott removed his warrant card and placed it down upon the countertop.

'We are detectives, Gladys. We normally work from Bristol, but today, we thought we'd come to your lovely little village.'

'Who is he?'

'That's what we are trying to find out. Have you heard the name Jesse Garcia before?'

'Nope.'

'He's an American.'

'Nope. Never heard of him. He's not from Hinton.'

'Are you sure?'

'Positive.'

'Could he be from the new estate?' McEwan asked.

Chilcott saw a grimace on Gladys's face at the mere mention of *the estate*.

'The pubs,' Chilcott said, 'do any of them open late?'

Gladys peered at Chilcott with her small silvery eyes. 'They close at eleven when they're meant to.'

Chilcott chuckled again. 'It's okay, Gladys. I'm not from licensing. There's nothing I like more than a cheeky lock-in myself.'

Gladys rolled her shoulders and hid behind her steaming mug.

'Do either of them have accommodation?'

'Yes. The Fox has rooms, but the Fleece doesn't. Bryan applied for them to have six guest rooms about ten years ago, but the council wouldn't allow it. Bloody unfair, if you ask me. Why should one be allowed and not the other?'

'I can't answer that, Gladys, but I'm sure it was a topic for hot debate.' Chilcott glanced mischievously at McEwan. 'Anyway,' he said, bringing Gladys back to the matter at hand. 'Do you know what time the Fox and Hounds opens?'

'Eleven.'

Chilcott looked at his watch. It was ten fifty-two.

'Fantastic. And do you know the name of the person I'd need to speak to there about guest rooms?'

'That would be Sandra. She's the landlady.'

'That's great, Gladys. You have been a great help. Can I just ask one last question, please?'

She looked at him with suspicion.

'Are you aware of anything *unusual* here in the last couple of days?'

'Like what?'

'Anything. Anything at all?'

'No.'

'No car crashes, or anyone getting injured?'

'No.'

'Okay. Thank you.'

Gladys fixed her stare on Chilcott as he fixed his jacket in readiness for the cold outside.

'Are you going to buy something, then?'

'Uh…' Chilcott looked to McEwan. 'Sean, do you need anything?'

McEwan shook his head.

'I think we're alright, thanks, Gladys.'

Her molten eyes peered up at Chilcott for a long moment.

'Tell you what,' Chilcott said, removing a folded five-pound note from inside a flap of his warrant card. 'I'll take some gum.'

He picked up a pack of chewing gum from the small display at the side of the counter and slid the note towards Gladys. 'Keep the change.'

'Are you sure, my lover? That's very decent of you.'

'I'm sure. Thanks for your help, Gladys.'

CHAPTER SEVEN

The conversation with Gladys hadn't taken the investigation any further, other than confirming to Chilcott that this was a village where even the slightest anomaly would stand out. Hinton Charterhouse was a proper village. A place not entirely locked in time, but a village where the locals were clearly proud of their heritage, and rightly so, which only made Garcia's case even more puzzling.

The Fox and Hounds Public House greeted them with a welcoming warmth from the wood-burning stove, and at just gone 11:00 a.m., Chilcott and McEwan were the only *customers*.

'Alright, my lovers?' the lady behind the bar said.

'Good morning,' Chilcott said glancing around the large open-plan bar area. Comfy seating was dotted around in no particular design other than to allow pockets of conversation to happen in a very homely setting.

'What can I get you, gentlemen?' the bar lady asked.

'Is it Sandra?'

'Yes,' the lady said with a questioning smile, this time taking more notice of their suits.

'We were given your name by lovely Gladys over in the shop.'

Sandra bobbed her head with a waning smile but didn't answer.

'My name is DI Robbie Chilcott, and this is my colleague, DC Sean McEwan.'

'Okay,' Sandra replied tentatively.

'There's nothing to worry about,' Chilcott said, approaching the bar counter. 'We are investigating an unusual event that happened in the village over the weekend, and we were wondering if you have any guests staying with you at the moment?'

Sandra's demeanour changed to one of concern. 'What sort of event. Do you mean a crime?' she said, seemingly appalled at the thought. 'We don't have crime here in Hinton.'

Chilcott opened his arms wide as a calming gesture. 'We still don't know,' he said. 'That's why we are here.'

Sandra gave the two detectives another once-over.

'Do you have any ID, a card or something?'

'Of course.' Chilcott nodded for McEwan to join him at the bar, and they both presented Sandra with their warrant cards.

'We usually work in Bristol,' Chilcott said. 'On major crimes.'

'Major crimes?'

'Like I said, I'm sure it's nothing to be concerned about.'

'What do you want from me?'

'A guest list. The names of anyone who has been staying here, maybe from Friday night onwards?'

'That will be easy. We only have one room booked out at the moment.'

'Do you happen to know the name of that guest?'

Sandra looked at the officers again, considering their request.

'Hold on,' she said, walking hastily away from the bar and into a back room and out of sight.

Chilcott flashed his lids at McEwan, and they waited for Sandra to return.

'Shall we grab a coffee while we're here, boss?' McEwan suggested.

'Not a bad idea, son. We could warm up a little by the fire and discuss what we've found out before we head out again.'

Sandra returned with a large leaf, landscaped, hard-backed book and opened the heavy-looking book on the bar top in front of the Chilcott and McEwan.

Chilcott took a cursory look down at the blank pages and decided a small A5 pad would probably do the job more efficiently.

Sandra ran a finger to the weekend dates. 'Mr and Mrs Jones were staying here on Saturday night. They left yesterday morning.'

'Mr and Mrs Jones, eh?' Chilcott said. 'And they left together?'

'Yes. We didn't see much of them, other than at meal times.'

'I bet. They probably needed to keep their energy up.'

Sandra stared at him blankly.

'Anyway,' Chilcott said, changing the subject quickly. 'Have you ever heard the name Garcia – Jesse Garcia?'

Sandra pouted and shook her head. 'Don't think so. Should I?'

'I don't know. Would you say you know most of the people in the village?'

'Yes. I'd have said that I know most of them, but I've never heard of anyone called Garcia. That sounds like a Spanish name.'

'He's American.'

'I'm not aware of any Americans living in the village.'

'Thank you, Sandra. While we're here, we thought we'd grab a couple of coffees, if possible, please?'

'Yes, of course.'

Sandra turned her back and began decanting freshly-ground coffee from a large stainless steel barista machine at the back of the bar.

'Take a seat somewhere,' she said. 'I'll bring them over.'

'Thanks,' Chilcott replied. 'We'll sit over by your lovely fire.' He made a point of looking around the empty bar lounge. 'Why not have one yourself, on me,' he said.

'Thank you. I will.'

Chilcott and McEwan shuffled over to the high-backed leather seats closest to the fire, and Chilcott pulled up a third chair alongside them.

'I've put the milk in a jug. Help yourselves to sugar,' Sandra said, bringing the drinks across to them.

Chilcott patted the seat next to him. 'Come and take a seat with us,' he said. 'It's so nice to be in a proper village pub again.'

Sandra looked a tad uncomfortable with the idea but did as instructed with a courteous, thank you.

'Hmmm, great-looking coffee. Thank you,' McEwan said, dropping two cubes of sugar into his bowl-like cup with a pair of delicate prongs, causing the coffee to spill out onto the saucer.

'Have you been landlady here for long?' Chilcott asked, taking a slurp from his cup.

'About twelve years now,' Sandra replied.

'Do many of the locals come into the pub?'

'Yes. We do a quiz night twice a week, Wednesdays and Sundays.'

'And you do okay from it?'

'Yes. They are very popular. This is a lovely community village. Everyone looks out for one another. Nothing is ever too much trouble if someone needs help. You know?'

Chilcott knew the concept, but sadly, for him, there was no such feeling of collectiveness on the housing estate in which he lived. He'd been there for nearly nine months now and still hadn't spoken to either of his neighbours and had probably only seen them twice in that time.

'That's good,' he said, taking another sip of coffee. 'What about the Fleece?'

'Bryan does okay too. He's right on the junction of the road, which isn't so great for him, but he still gets pretty good custom.'

Chilcott looked around the bar area again. 'Do you have CCTV?'

'We have quite limited CCTV, actually. It covers the till and entrance and the main hallway upstairs to the accommodation.'

'Are you good with faces?'

'I am. I don't always remember a name, but a face, I never forget.'

'If we showed you an image, would you mind taking a look?'

'Of course.'

Chilcott quickly muttered into McEwan's ear, 'Get on to custody. See if they can send you a link to Garcia's mug shot.'

McEwan stood up, took out his phone and walked to the far side of the room where he was less likely to be overheard.

'Is it bad, this event you are here for?' Sandra asked, watching DC McEwan speaking quietly on his phone.

'It might be,' Chilcott said. 'That's why we are taking this seriously.'

'Has someone died?'

'Why do you ask that?'

Sandra pointed a finger in Chilcott's direction. 'You're an inspector. You're both detectives. It doesn't take much to work out that something serious must have happened?'

Chilcott brushed lint from the cloth of his thighs and emitted a resigned sigh.

'We hope and pray it's nothing. I can't tell you too much for obvious reasons, but I think it only fair to keep you in the loop as best I can.'

Sandra leaned forwards, just as Chilcott expected. She wanted to know more. She *had* to learn more.

Chilcott wiped a hooked finger across his brow and looked behind his shoulder towards the door.

Sandra leaned closer still.

He licked his lips and leaned towards her himself. This had become their little secret.

'A man was picked up about half a mile down the road in the early hours of Sunday morning. He was only wearing boxer shorts, and there was some blood on him.'

Sandra's mouth widened as she listened with focussed concentration.

'His name is Jesse Garcia, or at least, that's what he's telling us.'

Sandra's eyes chased around Chilcott's face.

'We need to find out what happened here in Hinton Charterhouse and why Mr Garcia had blood on him?' Chilcott leaned back, breaking the secrecy of the conversation.

'Oh my, God!' Sandra said with her hand to her face.

'Okay,' DC McEwan said, returning to the table.

'Have you got it?' Chilcott asked.

'Yeah, no problem. I said it was for the incident board.'

'Good. Okay, Sandra. My colleague is going to show you a picture of the man I just told you about.'

DC McEwan gave Chilcott a sharp look.

'It's okay,' Chilcott said to McEwan. 'Sandra isn't a witness to the incident, so there will be no ID procedure issues from showing the image.'

McEwan looked sideways.

'I want you to take a really good look at his face,' Chilcott continued to Sandra. 'That's all you're going to see. Tell us if you recognise the man, and if so, where you recognise him from?'

Chilcott turned to McEwan and gestured for him to show Sandra the image.

McEwan handed her his phone and Chilcott watched her reaction as she brought the screen closer to her face. He could tell from her squinting eyes that she didn't recognise Garcia.

She shook her head and scowled. 'No. I can't say with any certainty that I've seen him around here before. Are you sure he was picked up down the road?'

McEwan gave Chilcott another concerned frown.

Chilcott slid a business card across the table. 'Give me a call if you hear anything that you think might help.'

'Yes, yes, of course. I'll mention it to my regulars.'

'You do that.'

Chilcott stood up and shook Sandra's hand. 'How much do I owe you for the coffees?'

'Oh, no, really. It's on the house.'

'Well, that's very kind of you, Sandra. Thank you. It has been lovely to meet you.'

DCI Foster paced the nine- or ten-step length of her office floor before turning and repeating the process. Chilcott and McEwan watched on in silence from the comfort of the soft *visitors'* chairs set back against the sidewall. Foster looked at her watch impatiently and then at Chilcott.

'He said to call back at three,' she said. 'What time do you make it?'

Chilcott slid back the sleeve of his shirt, exposing his watch face. 'It's still just before three,' he said, giving McEwan a twitch of the brow.

'That's it. I can't wait any longer,' Foster said, making a beeline for her desk phone. 'I need to know the results.'

She punched in the number taken from a yellow Post-it note and placed the phone on loudspeaker as she returned to pacing the floor.

'Forensic Laboratory Services,' the voice answered on the other end.

'Hello. This is Detective Chief Inspector Foster of Bristol major crime investigation team. Did I speak to you earlier?'

There was a short delay. 'Yes. You did, Ma'am.'

'And is there any update, please? You said to call back at three.'

'One moment, please.' The line clicked, and piped elevator music chimed through the speaker.

'Isn't that Art Garfunkel?' McEwan asked.

'Yeah, Trouble over Bridgwater,' Chilcott said. That had been an Avon and Somerset staple joke for decades.

'Hello, Ma'am,' the voice returned.

'Yes, go on.'

'We have emailed the results to CSI Melanie Sellars.'

'She's not here. She's based in Bath. Can you tell us what the results are, please?'

They looked at each other as the person on the other end of the line read through the results in a low, monotonous tone.

'We have two DNA profiles,' he said.

'Two profiles?' Foster questioned.

'Yes. Probably family members going by the similarities of the DNA.'

Foster stared wide-eyed at Chilcott.

'We are definitely talking about human DNA here?' she said.

'One hundred percent human DNA. No doubts. And neither appear on the database, so their identities are unknown.'

'Shit,' Foster said. 'Okay, can you forward that report to me as well, please? I sent you an email around two o'clock. You'll find my email address there.'

'Will do. Just give me a moment.'

The line clicked back to muffled elevator music.

'So, he got into a fight with his brother and got punched in the mouth for his troubles,' McEwan offered as a suggestion.

'That's possible,' Foster said. 'But his brother would have to be pretty badly injured given the amount of blood.'

'I'm not convinced,' Chilcott said, shaking his head.

'A bleeding mouth would be enough to mix the two blood samples,' McEwan said. 'It wouldn't take much, sir.'

'Hold on, here it is,' Foster said, bringing the forensic report onto the screen.

'And the brother could have a head injury,' McEwan continued. 'We all know how much blood can flow out of a head wound.'

'I still don't know,' Chilcott said. 'I'd have expected to see impact wounds on Garcia's fists or face; some sort of marks to show he'd been in a violent struggle. He had blood in his mouth at the hospital, but there was no mention of swelling or damaged teeth, which I'd expect to see.'

Foster stood back from the computer screen, her body rigid. 'It's not his brother.'

Chilcott and McEwan stopped talking and looked at the DCI.

'Ma'am?' McEwan said.

Foster slowly turned to face her colleagues.

'We've got female DNA – on both profiles.'

CHAPTER EIGHT

3:30 p.m.

A team of five detectives gathered in the second incident room of the Major Crime Investigation Team at Bristol. Their numbers would usually be greater. However, DI Chowdhury's street gang attack had absorbed the bulk of available detectives as tensions on the streets had swiftly escalated throughout the day.

Chilcott faced his small team alone. DCI Foster was unavailable due to complications with Chowdhury's investigation.

'Thanks for coming, team,' Chilcott said. 'You've probably already heard the updates through the grapevine. We have ourselves a bit of a case to sink our teeth into now. This is a live, ongoing concern, and I want you to down tools on whatever you are working on and put your energies into this for the next twenty-four hours or so.'

He paced back and forth in front of the detectives as they watched on.

'Limited evidence has been forthcoming through the day, and I can now confirm that the blood swabs taken from the suspect's skin at hospital do in fact, match that of two unknown female profiles. We believe these females are likely to be related due to the close similarities of the DNA profiles.'

Chilcott paused and rubbed an eye with the mid-joint of his index finger.

'Assuming we have two victims, we still have no idea who or where they are or anything about their current status.' He stopped and turned back, facing the small clutch of detectives. 'We must assume, given the extent of blood cleaned from the suspect, that they are both dead. Anything other than that final outcome is a bonus. But time is against us if we are to find them alive.'

Chilcott pulled the cover from a flip chart and tossed it to the floor. The next page displayed a blown-up line map of the Midford Valley, Hinton Charterhouse and outlying farmland. A thick black mark circled a wide perimeter within the map.

Chilcott tapped a red cross contained within the map. 'We know the suspect was picked up here.' He tapped the board again. 'A taxi driver was the first to call it in at 1:40 a.m., and an ambulance crew reached the suspect at 2:08 a.m., right here.' Chilcott banged the end of a marker pen on the red cross again. 'That's a minimum of thirty minutes between the first known sighting and point of pick up by the paramedics. We know Garcia was not injured, so we can assume that his ability to walk, or run, was unhindered.' Chilcott began slowly pacing again. 'Thirty minutes. Thirty minutes,' he repeated and stopped again. 'Any runners in the room?'

Two hands went up.

'How far could you get in bare feet in thirty minutes, Wes?'

'I usually do about six kilometres in thirty minutes, with trainers on, sir. So, bare feet; maybe cut that in half or more, depending on the surface?'

'It's a tarmac road – this road,' he said, knocking the line drawing with the butt end of the pen, making the detectives look at the diagram once again. 'So that means this boundary isn't too far off. The map shows a perimeter of three kilometres from where the ambulance picked up Garcia.'

Chilcott picked up the flip chart cover and held it over the top half of the circle.

'I think we can pretty much put the section I'm covering on the back-burners, as this is the direction in which we know Garcia was walking.' Chilcott tapped the bottom half of the circle. 'This is where we need to concentrate our resources in the first instance.'

He gave each of his detectives a firm look.

'We also know this is one of the quieter routes to and from Bath at this time of night. I have absolutely no hesitation in saying that someone else would have seen Garcia on this road that night – another taxi, a late-night reveller returning home with a friend, someone finishing a late shift, someone starting a very early morning shift. You get my drift. We need to find them, and we need to establish exactly where they saw Garcia in relation to this mark.' He jabbed at the red X again.

A hand went up.

'Yes.'

'What about the taxi driver, sir?'

'He's been spoken to, but uniformed officers said he was pretty vague. All we know is he saw Garcia in Hinton Charterhouse on the main road in the direction of Bath.'

'Did he have dash-cam, sir?'

'That's a good suggestion, Penny. But no, sadly, he did not.'

'Have we checked his social media, sir?' DC Wright asked.

'Unlike other investigations, we know very little about our suspect. We have a name – that's it – and we know he buys his underwear in Marks and Sparks. We've put his name through the system and tried it on Facebook, Twitter, Instagram, LinkedIn, you name it. We've got nothing other than what we believe to be his American heritage.'

Another hand went up, and Chilcott nodded.

'What about the embassy, boss. Is it worth a go?'

'That's an option open to us, but let's not make this an international incident until we absolutely have to.'

Chilcott looked at his team as the information sank in and was processed.

'We need every single one of the households shown within this perimeter boundary, visited and welfare checks made of all of them. I want to know the names of everyone you speak to, and I want to know where they were, what they heard and what they saw on Saturday night from 10 p.m. onwards.'

'There must be three hundred properties, boss,' one of the detectives said.

'Three hundred and twelve, to be exact. Most of which are located together along the main roads of Hinton Charterhouse.'

Chilcott could see the detectives looking unsettled as they shifted in their seats and murmured comments to one another.

'Don't worry,' he said. 'We're bringing in resources from the district, and we are pulling together a team of uniformed officers to help with the door-to-door enquiries. This is going to be a ball-ache, people. But we find ourselves in a situation we often seem to be, with time very much against us. I've spoken to the Force Incident Manager at Comms. I will be notified immediately if we receive any calls from the Hinton Charterhouse area with concerns for welfare. I'm sure it won't be long before someone reports a work colleague not turned up or someone not able to contact a relative or friend.'

A hand went up from one of the detectives.

'Yes.'

'Sir, has the hospital been checked for anyone living in the Hinton area being admitted with wounds consistent with that amount of blood loss?'

'Already checked. Negative result. But good thinking – keep it coming. Throw anything at me.'

Another hand went up.

'Go on.'

'What if he didn't walk, sir? What if he drove or someone else drove him. That boundary could be significantly larger.'

'There are more what-ifs than knowns at this time,' Chilcott said, looking at the map again. 'But we don't have the luxury to speculate. We can only work on the information we've got, which is sadly lacking. If and when that changes, we can then change our goalposts.'

'Was a dog sent out to track?' DC Chiba asked.

'Good question, Penny. As you may know, it was freezing on Saturday night. By all accounts, there was a cold clinging mist in the Hinton Charterhouse area. We had rain where I was. A dog was sent to track but only once we had suspicion the next morning. So effectively, too many hours had passed, and any scent was disturbed by the traffic movement. We also sent up a drone to check the embankment of the valley for any crashed vehicles that may have tumbled over the side, but there was nothing. And so, people, luck and hope are all we have to work with right now.'

'What about the suspect, sir?' DC Phillips asked.

'We have secured an extension of custody time limits, and we are going to interview Garcia again, now we have the forensic DNA results. He's going to be legally represented this time. Kevin Wilson is the duty solicitor allocated to Garcia's interview and I've already put him in the loop. We're lucky; Kev is a sensible bloke. If Garcia has information he's withholding, I'm sure Kev will make him do the right thing. Okay,' Chilcott said, clapping his hands together loudly. 'Sean and Fleur, get yourselves interview ready. The rest of you, phone home; you're not making it back for tea tonight.'

CHAPTER NINE

6:32 p.m.

Jesse Garcia and Kevin Wilson entered the interview room. There was an air of defiance about Garcia that wasn't present during the first encounter.

DC McEwan got the legal pleasantries out of the way and then got straight down to matter in hand.

'Mr Garcia. I'm sure your legal advisor has informed you about the DNA results obtained from the blood swabs taken from you at the Royal United Hospital. This is your chance to account for how the blood of two females is found present upon your semi-naked body?'

'Uh… my client has written a prepared statement,' Mr Wilson said. 'Uh… if I may read it out on behalf of my client, please?'

McEwan opened his hand. 'Please do, Mr Wilson.'

'I, Jesse Garcia of Tampa Heights, Florida, would like to assist the police in their investigation into the circumstances surrounding my presence on the B3110 Midford Road, Bath, in the early hours of Sunday the sixth of March. I have been asked several times to account for my presence at that location, and for my physical presentation at that time. Specifically, I am being asked to account for my semi-naked state, the apparent smearing of blood on my body, and the location from which I came. I am unable to answer any of these questions at this time.' Mr Wilson gave McEwan a subtle shake of the head and continued. 'Signed, Jesse Garcia. Monday the seventh of March at six-twelve p.m.'

DC McEwan blinked at Mr Wilson for a few seconds.

'Is that it?' he asked.

'These are my instructions. My client will be answering no comment to all other questions at this time.'

McEwan balled a fist and banged it on the table. He kept his fist tightly clenched.

'You have the blood of two females on your body,' he said through gritted teeth. 'This is not an everyday occurrence. Finding someone walking alone in their boxer shorts, in the middle of the night, in a remote location, is not an everyday occurrence. You know what happened leading up to the point you were found. Now, do the right thing and tell us everything you possibly can about it.'

'I am afraid my client will be answering no comment to all other questions,' Mr Wilson said apologetically.

McEwan sat back in his chair, his mouth ajar.

'Who does the blood belong to?' DC Phillips asked, becoming the calming voice of reason.

'No comment,' Garcia replied in a deadpan American accent.

'Where are those people now?'

'No comment.'

'How did their blood get to be on your person?'

'No comment,' he said in a monosyllabic tone.

'We know the blood found on your body belongs to two different females, possibly of the same family. Who are they?'

'Uh, I think you've already asked my client who the blood belongs to, and he has provided his reply,' Mr Wilson said.

Phillips shot Wilson a glare and continued. 'Why were you only wearing underwear?'

'No comment.'

'Where are the rest of your clothes?'

'No comment.'

'What were you doing on the B3110 Midford Road at between one and two in the morning of Sunday the sixth of March?'

'No comment.'

Phillips turned to McEwan and gave a slight twitch of the mouth.

'Mr Garcia, I am investigating an offence of murder. I am asking you to account for the presence of blood belonging to two unknown females found on your semi-naked body,' McEwan said, taking over again. 'I believe this fact may be due to your having taken part in the commission of the offence in question. If you fail, or refuse to account for the fact about which you are being questioned a court may draw a proper inference from that failure or refusal. A record is being made of this interview and it may be given in evidence if you are brought to trial.'

McEwan stared at Garcia for a long moment. 'Is that understood?'

'Yeah, man.'

'Go on then, tell me what that means.'

Garcia pouted and rubbed his nostrils with the end of a finger. He cocked his head and stared back at McEwan.

'You want me to tell you about the blood.'

'And if you don't?'

Garcia leaned his head back and yawned. 'Whatever.'

'A court can draw inference from your failure to answer.'

'Like I said. Whatever.'

'This is your opportunity to tell me everything you know about the blood.'

Garcia slowly folded his arms and sat in defiant silence.

'Are you refusing to answer my Special Warning?'

'No comment.'

McEwan bit his lip and turned to Phillips who shook her head.

'The time is 6:53 p.m. That is the end of the special warning and this interview is concluded.'

McEwan stomped out of the interview room and found Chilcott striding towards him.

'Did you hear that, boss?' McEwan fumed.

'I did.'

'It's bollocks, boss.'

'It is. Leave it with me.'

Chilcott bounded onwards and saw Mr Wilson strolling along the cellblock corridor away from him.

'Kev, can I have a private word, please?' Chilcott said.

Chilcott opened the door to an empty consultation room

and held it for Mr Wilson to walk inside. He closed the door and rubbed his face.

'Kev – you know where Sean was coming from in there?'

'Of course, I do, but I can't go behind the law.'

'Kev, we've known each other a long time. When have I ever pulled a fast one over you?'

'Do you really want me to answer that?'

'Come on – seriously.'

'I am being serious. My client does not have to answer any Special Warning questions when you, *the police*, have not established an offence has been committed.'

'We have reasonable grounds to suspect a serious offence has been committed due to the presence of two sources of blood on that man. Reasonable grounds are all we need to pursue a line of investigation. And that's what we have.'

'Enough to arrest and interview, I agree. But not enough to draw inference from my client's silence. He has provided a prepared statement—'

'Which was utter nonsense. He just repeated what was asked of him. He hasn't provided any form of account whatsoever.'

Mr Wilson breathed in slowly and perched down on the edge of the table.

'Robbie, I wish I could help you. I really do. But…'

'Did he say anything to you at all about how the blood got on him?'

'I can't breach client confidentiality.'

'I'm not asking you to breach anything. Just throw me a fricking bone.'

Mr Wilson shrugged and clamped his jaw firmly shut.

Chilcott checked back over his shoulder and leaned in closer to Wilson. 'Kev, I've got nothing to go on. Nothing.'

'I'm afraid that's not my problem, Robbie. And that's certainly not Mr Garcia's problem either.'

'What if it was your wife, Kev? What if it was your daughter?'

Mr Wilson stood up from the table and walked back towards the door, before pausing next to Chilcott.

'I hear you, Rob. But it's not. It's not.'

CHAPTER TEN

Tuesday 8th March

7:50 a.m.

Eight hours twenty-eight minutes until Garcia could be released from custody without charge – a free man.

Chilcott stared up at the scant whiteboard of Incident Room 2. He hadn't enjoyed a good night's sleep as the puzzle of the American raged in his mind. His head throbbed with a lack of sleep and an overindulgence of caffeine. By this stage of an investigation, he would typically have had at least several significant lines of enquiry to help join the dots, but there was nothing. The timeline of events was muddled; unusually, finding the suspect was his starting point. But without a crime scene and a victim, figuring out the MO was like completing a jigsaw with the missing central pieces. But he also had the tantalising prospect of the two unknown blood samples. Who were they? And where would he find them? His eyes searched the white empty spaces of the timeline. It was already looking increasingly likely that his only option was to go to press. He didn't like involving the media so soon into an investigation. It smacked of desperation. But given what little he had to go on, there was no other choice.

The team re-assembled at nine in the briefing room. This time the DCI and other uncommitted detectives had joined them.

'Good morning, everyone,' Chilcott said, stepping forward to the front of the stacked briefing room. 'It's not often I say this at such an early stage of an investigation, but we've reached a stalemate. Garcia isn't talking, and without any other significant lines of enquiry, we must decide how we now proceed. We are going to cut this as fine as we can and apply for a magistrate's extension of custody time limits at the very last moment. That will afford us the maximum time to investigate Garcia.'

He focussed on several of the detectives. 'That means by four-eighteen this afternoon, we either have more time to question Garcia, or he walks out of the custody unit a free man, and there isn't a single person in this room who is going to allow that to happen. I'm going to ask you all to phone home after briefing. We are going to work on this problem until we get answers. No one leaves until that time. I know some of you are also involved in the street gang stabbing. We've spoken to DI Chowdhury, and he is in full agreement that you are now working on this case if you can be spared. If Garcia has injured or killed someone, we cannot afford for him to be released because we've failed in our due diligence to investigate properly.'

He paused and looked at the team again. It was a big ask, but they were professionals and highly-trained detectives, and that, he concluded, was the only card he held.

'I'm not going to stand here and tell you what to do because the simple answer is, I don't know myself.'

He noticed several detectives looking at one another.

'We are preparing a press release, but it's important that we don't alarm the public at this stage. However, it's now over fifty hours since Garcia was picked up. That means it's also at least fifty hours since he potentially maimed or killed. Somebody has to be missing from someone's life in whatever capacity that may be, and that's our way in. We have to know who that blood belongs to, and the public response to a press release could be our ticket. Without that information and alongside Garcia's silence, we're stuffed. And so, I put it over to you guys. This is an open forum. No matter how stupid you may think it is, any suggestion could be the key to opening up this case. So please, let's do this together. Away you go.'

Chilcott stepped back and sat down next to the DCI. They watched together as the team of detectives shuffled in their seats, some in whispered conversation with the colleagues who sat next to them.

A hand went up from DC Penny Chiba.

'No need for hands, Penny. Just let it out,' Chilcott said and stood up next to the whiteboard with the marker pen poised in his hand.

'We've already checked the hospitals, but what about the

GPs. Someone may have come in with deep lacerations or something?' she said.

'Good. But where do we draw the boundary lines?' Chilcott said.

'Frome to Bath?' another officer suggested.

'That sounds reasonable, but we're probably talking about thirty GP surgeries, including all those in Frome and Bath. Identify those in between and work outwards from there.'

'I'll do it,' DC Chiba said. 'I'll get a list drawn up and phone around.'

'Good. Thanks, Penny. Any other ideas, anyone?'

'What about wider taxi firms. They operate all through the night. A driver may have noticed Garcia in a different location, such as Norton St Phillip, or even further afield, like Faulkland. We're assuming Garcia stuck to the main roads, but what if he came from one of the minor roads? We may be focusing on the wrong place?'

'Agreed, but I think it's unlikely. I'd hope most people would call in seeing a half-naked bloke covered in blood. If he'd come from further afield, he'd have been on the road for well over an hour before being spotted by our taxi driver, and I just can't see that being the case.'

'Or, they'd drive on as quickly as possible assuming someone else had reported it.'

DCI Foster nodded her agreement at the comment.

'Which is why we intend to go to press. Anyone else?' Chilcott asked.

'We know the suspect has no visible injuries. What if the victim isn't a victim? What if they were bled willingly,' DC Rees asked.

'Go on.'

'I'm thinking some sort of cult or weirdo-stuff like that?'

'It's possible. Anything's possible. But where do we start looking for weirdo-stuff like that?'

'On the internet?'

'Okay. Can you look into that for us, please, Rees?'

'Sir?' a timid voice came from towards the back of the room.

'Yes. Don't stand on ceremony, just shout it out.'

'Uh… isn't Jesse Garcia a fictional character, sir?'

The room fell silent instantly, and all faces turned towards the back of the room.

'What was that?' Chilcott asked. 'Stand up, would you, please?'

A female detective stood up from the back row.

'What did you just say – he's a fictional character?'

'Yes, sir. I'm fairly sure there was a West End show with a character called Jesse Garcia.'

Chilcott looked at DCI Foster, who pulled a nonplussed face and shrugged.

'Are you into theatre shows, Amy?'

'When I can, sir.'

'What do you know about this show, with Jesse Garcia in it?'

'It's a crime thriller, sir. Set in Miami.'

Chilcott held his breath. His eyes burned wide upon the detective standing up at the back of the room.

Jesus Christ!

'Come and see me after the briefing, Amy. Tell me everything you know about this show and Jesse Garcia's character.'

'Yes, sir.'

A tap at the door interrupted Chilcott's internet search.

'Come in, Amy. Close the door, would you, please.'

DC Amy Fowler did as instructed and took a seat near Chilcott.

'You're right,' he said. 'I've just been looking it up. Jesse Garcia is the anti-hero in the theatre show.'

'Miami Heat,' sir.

'Yes, that's right. But what I don't understand is why our Garcia is saying that is his name? That's why we couldn't bloody find him on our system – he's a sodding fictional character.'

'I'm fairly sure the show is doing the rounds, sir.'

'What do you mean?'

'It's a touring company, sir. They completed at the West End towards the end of last year.'

'Hold on, so the show is touring the country?'

'I believe so, sir.'

Chilcott quickly tapped the keyboard, waited, and flopped back in his seat when the information populated his screen. 'I don't believe it; they were in Bath from Wednesday to Saturday last week.'

'At the Theatre Royal, sir?'

Chilcott looked at DC Fowler with a mesmerising smile. 'Yes. This is unreal.'

'It's my favourite theatre, sir.'

'It's my favourite theatre now too. How do we find out more about the touring group?'

'Um, type the show into the search engine, and it should tell you where the company has moved on to.'

Chilcott did as requested.

'Regent Theatre, Stoke-on-Trent,' he said, his eyes darting around the screen. 'Right,' he said after a few seconds of reading the details. 'Amy, I want you to phone the Theatre Royal in Bath. Just confirm that they had the show there on Saturday night and tell them that we will be coming over to look at their CCTV, so I want someone there to meet us who can work it. Explain this is a matter of utmost urgency. Any problems, let me know.'

'Yes, sir.'

'I'll meet you down in the car park in twenty minutes.'

'Um, yes, sir.'

Chilcott strode with a renewed vigour into the incident room, took a thick black marker pen and wrote **FICTIONAL CHARACTER** beneath Jesse Garcia's name.

CHAPTER ELEVEN

Having called ahead, DC Fowler had arranged for them to meet the theatre's director, Harvey Samways, in its foyer at 10:30 a.m.

It had been a good few years since Chilcott was last in this part of Bath. Many streets had been pedestrianised as part of city centre anti-pollution improvements. That meant they had to park what felt like miles away and make the rest of the journey on foot, but at least it was dry and sunny.

They entered the grand foyer doors of the old theatre building and went across to the Box Office desk, where a staff member was seated behind the booth.

'Hi,' Chilcott said. 'We are from the police. We're here to meet Mr Samways. He knows we're coming.'

'Oh, yes. Hold on a moment, please.'

The staff member called a number, and a man bounded into the foyer several minutes later down a deep red-carpeted stairway.

'Hello, hello,' he chirped. 'Harvey Samways – I'm the director of this wonderful old theatre.'

'Good afternoon, sir,' Chilcott said, shaking his hand. 'DI Robbie Chilcott, and this is my colleague, DC Amy Fowler.'

'Welcome. Welcome,' Mr Samways said with open arms. 'I understand you have some questions?'

'Yes, if that's possible. We really shouldn't keep you too long.'

'No, not at all. Not at all. Come on through with me.'

Mr Samways walked them back up the red-carpeted stairway and into a side office.

'Would either of you care for a drink? Coffee perhaps?'

'No, thank you. But that's very kind,' Chilcott said.

'So, how may I be of assistance to you both?' Mr Samways asked.

'You had a show here last week,' Chilcott paused, turning to DC Fowler.

'Miami Heat,' she added.

'Ah, yes. A spectacular production. Did either of you see it?'

'Uh, no, sadly not. But we are interested in the show. Would you happen to have a flyer or brochure hanging around from last week, please?'

'Yes, yes, of course. We have probably got a half-box of programmes left over. They haven't been thrown away yet as we often get fans in – just like you two. I'll be back in a skip and a jump.'

Mr Samways beamed with a proud smile and left them both in the small office.

'A skip and a jump? Is that a *lovey* thing?' Chilcott asked Fowler.

'Beats me, sir. I think he's just happy in his work.'

'I'm glad one of us is.'

'Here we go,' Mr Samways said, coming back into the room. 'I've actually got some signed copies. We would normally charge twenty-five pounds each for these, but I don't mind if you'd like to take one copy away with you… so long as you promise to come back and support us another time.'

'That's lovely, thank you,' DC Fowler said. 'I will certainly be coming back. This is my favourite theatre.'

'Oh, how wonderful to hear. And what about you, Detective Inspector? Do you enjoy the theatre?'

'I can't say that I have been much… recently. But I'm certainly no stranger to drama.'

'Of course. You must experience all sorts of exciting things in your line of work.'

'We certainly do. On that note, would your brochure happen to have a breakdown of the characters and maybe a synopsis of this *Miami Heat* show?'

'Yes, of course.'

Mr Samways thumbed his way through the pages.

'We have a breakdown of each of the main character actors, their portfolios and career highlights, including any television or film productions they have starred in.'

Chilcott gave DC Fowler a small wink. 'That's great,' he said, not really giving a damn about celebrity status. 'How about the character, Jesse Garcia?'

Mr Samways swayed his finger back and forth in Chilcott's direction.

'I might have guessed that you would be interested in the naughty ones.' Mr Samways laughed heartily to himself. 'Never off duty, eh?'

Chilcott watched as Mr Samways flicked several pages backwards and held the glossy magazine towards Chilcott's face.

'Travis Yardley,' Mr Samways said. 'And what a spectacular performance it was. Do you know, he was originally an understudy? Thankfully, we had enough time to print these brochures, especially to include Mr Yardley, and I'm so glad we did. He absolutely stole the show... oops, no pun intended.' Mr Samways broke into another hoot of laughter.

Chilcott took the brochure from Mr Samways, turned it around to see a one-page spread of Travis Yardley, and his chest plummeted.

'That's him,' he muttered.

'That's right, Travis Yardley. What a great future this young man has, considering he was on stage alongside established West End and television stars. His performance was absolutely magnificent – such a menacing, emotional depth to his portrayal of Jesse Garcia.'

'He's an actor,' Chilcott whispered to himself.

Mr Samways leaned forwards. 'Uh... Inspector?'

'Where does Travis Yardley live. Is he local?' Chilcott asked, snapping out of his thoughts.

'Gosh, no. I'd imagine he's from the London area, most likely.'

Chilcott frowned.

'His agent will have contact details for him. I can find out who that is if it helps?'

'Yes. Please. That would be a huge help.'

'I'll be back in a skip and a—'

'Jump?' Chilcott finished the sentence.

'Ha, ha, you've got my number already, Inspector.' Mr Samways beamed warmly and left the room again.

Chilcott looked down at the brochure. Garcia's face stared back at him from a full-page spread.

'You're a fucking actor,' Chilcott muttered.

Mr Samways re-appeared a few moments later with a number for *Tread the Boards Talent Agency* and a separate contact number for the performance director of the theatre company.

'Thank you, Mr Samways.'

'Please – call me Harvey.'

'You have no idea what a help you have been today, Harvey.'

'Oh,' Mr Samways said bashfully, 'anything for our brave boys and girls.'

'Your CCTV…' Chilcott cut over him. 'What does it show of the actors after each performance ends?'

'Oh, well, obviously nothing from the changing areas, that just wouldn't do. But we do have some coverage backstage. By the lockers and on the exits and entrance to the theatre building.'

'What time would this company have finished on Saturday night?'

'Oh, the stage crew would have been here until about 1 a.m. They had to clear the stage and load the lorries for the next leg of their tour.'

'What about the actors?'

'Hmmm.' Mr Samways pondered his thoughts for a moment. 'Some stayed to have a meal with myself, my wife, and a few of the other staff. But most actors went their own ways.'

'What about Travis Yardley?'

'He wasn't with my party, though I'd have loved him to stay. No, he left fairly soon after the performance, from my recollection. I was rather disappointed. I'd have enjoyed a lengthy natter.'

'Where would he go – through the front theatre doors?'

'Oh no. No, no, no. Performers leave via a separate exit. No, we can't have them leaving with the audience. That simply wouldn't do.'

'Which exit would he have used?'

'It's on the side of the building onto St John's Place. I can show you if you like?'

'That would be fantastic. May I?' Chilcott said, holding the glossy brochure.

'By all means. That's your copy to do with whatever you please.'

They followed Mr Samways through to the auditorium and up the steps at the side of the grand stage. A large burgundy and gold velvet curtain hung feet from the edge of the raised stage.

Chilcott paused and looked out. 'Wow, that's a lot of seats.'

'Nine hundred on the dot. Have you ever fancied giving it a go, Inspector?'

'Not a hope. I'd fluff my lines.'

'You say that, but you'd be surprised how many established actors still worry about their lines right up until the moment they deliver them.'

'It's not for me,' Chilcott said.

'I'd love to give it go,' DC Fowler said.

'Then you must,' Mr Samways encouraged. 'There

might be a superstar in the making somewhere under that suit.'

'Right, shall we…' Chilcott said, holding out his arm in an attempt to bring the conversation back to the job in hand.

'So, this is where the actors change,' Mr Samways said, leading Chilcott and DC Fowler along a narrow and confined dusty corridor. 'And these are the lockers where they store their belongings. That's the camera I mentioned,' he said, pointing to a wall-mounted fixed lens. 'And just through here, excuse the trip hazards,' he said, stepping over several large piles of rolled fabric scenery. 'Is the side exit where many of our actors leave at the end of each performance.'

'Can we go outside?' Chilcott asked.

'I'll just check the door is unlocked. Yes, there we go.' Mr Samways opened the door, and daylight flooded into the dark and dusty exit.

Chilcott stepped outside and down onto the pavement. He was standing at the side of the theatre with a narrow thoroughfare running between the theatre building and boutique shops and restaurants on the other side. Fixed to the wall, he saw another simple CCTV camera facing the side exit and towards the back of the theatre. He looked around, studying the environment. There were no other council cameras in this immediate vicinity.

'Can we have the footage from Saturday night, please? From the time of the final curtain until, maybe, midnight?'

'I will ask someone to copy that for you. Um… can I just ask…?'

'Fire away.'

'You haven't actually said why you are interested in all of this.'

'Haven't we? I'm sorry about that. We have an interest in Travis Yardley. That's about all I can say.'

'Along with a great many other people, I can tell you,' Mr Samways gleamed.

Not as much as me, Chilcott said to himself. *Not as much as me*. 'Right, shall we go and grab that CCTV?'

CHAPTER TWELVE

They took the burnt CCTV footage to the local police station at Falcon Road, found an unused computer in the CID office and trawled through the disk. Concentrating from 10 p.m. onwards, DC Fowler was looking for all actors leaving the side exit, as Chilcott read the theatre brochure in more detail.

'You never told me it was so gruesome,' he said, having read the plot. 'Proper Hannibal Lecter stuff, this.'

'Yes, it is about a man who murders and then eats the body parts of his victims.'

'There's nothing like a light and fluffy theatre show to spend a hard-earned Saturday night's entertainment.'

Chilcott looked around the office. DS Reynolds and his team were head down, working through a local job.

'I'm just going for a slash a minute,' he said to DC Fowler, who gave him a stale expression.

'Probably more than you needed to know?'

'Uh ha,' DC Fowler said.

Chilcott found the gents toilet in the nearby corridor

and proceeded to relieve himself. But as he stared at the white-painted walls, inches from his face, an image of Garcia eating body parts flashed into his mind. He quickly finished the job in hand and burst back out into the office, doing up his zipper as he went.

'Someone get me the custody centre on the phone right now,' he said.

DS Reynolds and his team looked at Chilcott as if he was talking a different language.

'Someone get me onto Keynsham custody unit. You guys know the number. Come on…'

DS Reynolds did the honours, albeit slightly reluctantly, and handed Chilcott the phone at the end of a fully-extended arm.

'Hello,' Chilcott said. 'Is this the custody sergeant? This is DI Chilcott. We have Jesse Garcia in the cells with you.'

'That's right. His solicitor has been—'

'Yeah. Yeah. Yeah. Don't worry about the solicitor right now.'

'He's been requesting an update.'

'Has Garcia taken a dump since he's been with you?'

The detectives around the table stopped what they pretended to be doing, and each of them stared at Chilcott.

'I'm sorry?' the custody sergeant said.

'Has Garcia taken a dump? It's a simple enough question.'

'I would imagine so, but there no need to be so—'

'Block the toilet. Stop him from flushing anything else away.'

'I'm sorry – this isn't a drugs job. You can't impinge on someone's liberty like that.'

'Just listen to what I'm saying. Block the toilet and monitor everything that passes through him. If it doesn't look like chicken curry, I want to know about it, okay?'

The line was silent.

'Sergeant, is that understood?'

'I'm not comfortable taking the prisoner's liberties away just like that—'

'You can, and you will. I'll be over shortly with my interview team. If you want to involve the superintendent, fill your boots. And then get them to phone me while you're at it.'

Chilcott slammed the phone down, and the team of Bath detectives faked going back to their business.

'What if he doesn't have the curry, boss?' DS Reynolds grinned.

'I know what I'm doing,' Chilcott said, as much to himself as anyone else. He looked around the table at the puzzled faces peering back at him.

'As you were.'

Chilcott walked back towards DC Fowler and sat down alongside her.

'Anything?' he asked.

'I think I've got Travis Yardley leaving the theatre at 10:21 p.m. It's quite busy outside the side door with people hanging around. There's a bit of jostling with fans clambering to get signing autographs. We see him walk off camera for a bit, but then we see him walking back into the shot a few moments later alongside a female.'

'Where? Let me see that.' Chilcott dragged a seat next to DC Fowler and leaned in closer to the computer monitor.

He watched the footage play out, just as DC Fowler had described.

'Who's that girl?' he asked.

'I don't know, sir.'

'Is she an actress?'

'I don't know, sir. I didn't see her leave via the side entrance.'

Chilcott got as close to the screen as possible without losing his focus. He prodded the screen with a finger.

'That's our victim. That's our girl. Great work, Amy. Keep a note of those times, and let's get this copied back at major crime. We have to track them. We have to know where they went from here.'

Chilcott leapt up from the chair and went back to DS Reynolds and his team.

'I need an urgent CCTV request from the city centre cameras – how do I do that?'

'If you know what cameras you're after, we can send someone down for you. If you like?'

'Can one of you come and look at this, please? Your local knowledge is better than mine.'

DS Reynolds followed Chilcott back to DC Fowler's computer and watched a replay of the footage.

'Okay. That'll be the Monmouth Place camera first and foremost, and then it looks as if they are headed in the direction of Kingsmead Square. Depending on their direction from there, you might need any number of other camera locations.'

'Do you have a body free to help me, please? It's really important – a life and death scenario.'

'Of course. Anything to help our major crime team brethren.'

DS Reynolds called out to one of his team, and an unwilling volunteer carried his carcass slowly across the office.

'Yeah,' he said.

'I need you to help DI Chilcott with some urgent CCTV,' DS Reynolds said.

The officer turned back towards his table like a sullen teenager who had just been asked to tidy up his room.

'But I'm—'

'Not any more you're not, son. You're working for me for the next few hours.'

'But…'

'No buts, Freddie,' DS Reynolds said. 'You've got a good local knowledge of the CCTV cameras, and our esteemed colleagues need our help.'

'Bu—'

Chilcott wheeled over a chair and placed the officer down into it before he had time to complain further.

'Take a look at this, would you, please?'

Chilcott landed a heavy hand on the young DC's shoulder.

'This could go well for your CV, son. Thanks for offering to help.'

The DC looked up at Chilcott like he'd just been had over in a game of cards.

'Take a close look at these two people,' Chilcott said. Touching them with a finger on the screen. 'Follow them. Tell me where they go and what cameras we need to follow their progress on.' He pressed play and studied the sullen DC as he stared grudgingly at the screen.

Chilcott tapped the glass where the suspect and the female were walking away. 'These two,' he said. 'Keep an eye on these two. We need to know exactly where they went and at what time.'

The officer sat silently with rounded shoulders until he finished the short CCTV clip.

'They've gone down Monmouth Street towards Kingsmead Square,' the detective said.

'That's what your skipper told me, but how do we get that footage? I need to see every single step taken by these two people.'

'We'd have to go to Lewis House where they record the footage.'

Chilcott held out an outstretched arm. 'After you, amigo. You know this place better than me.'

Soon after, they were inside the blackened inner rooms of Lewis House. The room was barely lit, aside from the light emitted from the thirty or more large TV monitors taking up an entire wall. Three CCTV operators sat behind a bank of desk-mounted single monitors, each with a hand-controlled joystick.

'Watcha, Freddie. Who are your mates?' one of the camera operators asked. His legs were hooked up on the chair next to him, and he lounged back like he was watching Netflix on a Friday night after a long week at the office.

'Uh, this is—'

'I'm Detective Inspector Chilcott from Bristol major crime, and this is my colleague, DC Fowler.'

Chilcott watched the legs of the camera operator slowly but purposefully lower to the floor.

'Oh. Hello, sir,' he said.

'Don't mind me. You look rushed off your feet.'

The operator rubbed the side of his face and looked intently at the screen in front of him. It showed a park with what looked like a toilet block and a collection of well-established trees nearby.

'Something exciting?' Chilcott asked him.

'Me? Oh, no. Uh, sir.'

Chilcott nodded and looked at the other two operators gawping at him rather than watching the screens.

'We need some help,' Chilcott said. 'Freddie here is going to ask you to access the files from Saturday night into Sunday morning. We are interested in the theatre area, and…' he looked at the district detective constable to help him out with the location names.

'Kingsmead Square,' Freddie said.

'Got a request slip?' one of the other operators asked.

'Excuse me?' Chilcott answered.

'Can't do nothing until we've got a request slip. And then it will have to be prioritised with the other stuff we've got.' The second operator jabbed a finger in the direction of an in-tray stacked full of paper requests.

'Shall I go out and come in again?' Chilcott asked. 'I seem to have come into the fucking Twilight Zone or something here.'

'The what?' the first operator asked.

'Forget it.'

Chilcott turned to the district DC. 'Do you know how to use these machines?'

'Yeah, no probs, boss. I use them all the time.'

'He can't,' the second operator spoke over them. 'He's not allowed.'

Chilcott stepped forwards and closed the gap between himself and the second operator. He bent down looking at the single screen showing an empty alleyway beside a partially-filled car park. Chilcott leaned a fist on the table beside the scruffy young waste of his oxygen.

'I tell you what, sunshine. You'd better start helping me, or I'll make your life so fucking difficult; you'll be begging me to put you out of your misery.'

'You can't—'

'Try me,' Chilcott glared.

The young man scratched nervously at the side of his unkempt mop of hair and looked back at the third, as yet, silent CCTV operator.

'Just do the bloody request,' the third operator said to his headstrong colleague.

Assuming he was the most senior operator present, Chilcott went over to speak to him.

'Can you get me onto the Kingsmead Square camera on Saturday night from…'

Chilcott looked to DC Fowler to provide him with the details.

'Ten twenty-seven, sir,' she said.

'Give a tolerance of five minutes,' Chilcott instructed. 'We don't know how accurate the theatre CCTV time is on our baseline footage.'

The third operator tapped a keyboard, and the image changed on the largest screen of the bank of cameras.

'What are we looking at?' Chilcott asked.

'That's Kingsmead Square,' the third operator said.

'All I can see is a big tree and two homeless bums fighting over a fag butt on the floor.'

'The camera's on pre-set. It'll swing around in a second.'

Sure enough, the camera quickly swung by about ninety degrees and, at the same time, zoomed in closer to a corner cafe and a small row of shops.

'Still on pre-set?' Chilcott asked.

'Yeah, I'm just checking the event log. We weren't alerted to anything on the Kingsmead Square camera until two-twelve on Sunday morning; a fight between three males.'

'So, it's pot luck if we see the people we're interested in?'

'Pretty much. If you'd phoned through and told us at the time what we were looking for, we could have overridden the pre-set and had a good old rummage around.'

'If only we knew at the time,' Chilcott murmured. 'My job would be a whole lot simpler.'

'As Simon was saying earlier, we would normally have a request slip with a description of who you're after.'

'Yeah, well. Serious and complex crime tends not to wait for convenient moments.'

'Do you know who you're looking for?'

'A male and female. He's about five-ten, slim build, shoulder-length dark brown hair. All in all, a smarmy-looking bastard. If he smiles, we'll probably notice the glow before anything else. She's shorter, has long brown hair halfway down her back and wearing a long brown winter coat. We haven't seen her face yet, so I can't tell you anything about that.'

'What have they done?'

Chilcott broke away from the screen, which was still changing camera angle every thirty seconds or so. He stared at the third camera operator.

'Nothing… yet. Where is the theatre in relation to this?' he asked.

Freddie stepped beside the screen and pointed with his hand. 'Up there, boss. This road is Monmouth Street.'

'Okay. So, they should be walking down somewhere between the Sainsbury's Local and the coffee shop?'

'That's right.'

'What time are we showing now?'

'Ten twenty-six,' the third operator said.

'Hold on,' Freddie said, 'pause here.'

Chilcott stepped forwards. 'That's them,' he said. 'Amy, take a note of the time.'

'Yes, sir,' DC Fowler duly complied.

'Okay, carry on,' Chilcott ordered.

The TV monitor came into life again, and Chilcott watched with clenched fists as they crossed the road towards the coffee shop. And with that, the camera swung again, and they were lost to view.

'Fuck it!' Chilcott shouted. 'Bollocks. Bollocks. Bollocks.'

'Pre-set camera,' the third operator stated, much to Chilcott's annoyance.

'No shit, Sherlock. Right, where could they be going?'

'They could be going through the square in one of three directions. Or towards the kebab shop. Or the chippy, which doesn't shut until eleven…'

Chilcott turned to the rotund third operator and looked down at the bottom hem of his polo shirt, which left about four inches of visible blubber between itself and the top of the man's jeans.

'Good chips… are they?'

'The best,' the man said, licking his lips.

'Where else could they be going,' Chilcott asked facing the screen once more.

'There's a Chinese restaurant—'

'Okay, let's assume for a moment that they aren't going for something to eat. What else is there? Did I see a couple of bars?'

'Yeah.'

Chilcott caught Freddie's eye and shook his head.

'Pause there, boss,' DC Fowler said from behind Chilcott.

The image froze, and they all looked closer to the screen.

'What did you see, Amy?' Chilcott asked.

'I thought I saw the back of him going through that red door.'

Freddie pointed. 'This one?' he said.

'Yes.'

'Just go back a few seconds. Let's see if we see more of them,' Freddie said to the operator.

The camera went in reverse, and together they all said, 'There.'

The camera moved frame by frame in a forwards direction.

'What's that place called?' Chilcott asked.

'Pippa's,' Freddie said. 'It's a sort of late opening lounge bar.'

'Is it open now?'

'Yeah, should be, boss.'

'Good. Run me a copy of this tape from ten twenty-five until this time, please. We're going to Pippa's, and when we know what time they left, we're coming back again — without a request slip.'

'No problem,' the third operator said.

Chilcott gestured for the other detectives to join him, and together, they left for Kingsmead Square.

CHAPTER THIRTEEN

Soft, trendy music played in the background as they walked with the manageress and business namesake, *Pippa*, into a back office.

'Nice place you've got here,' Chilcott said.

'Thank you. We've been here for seven months, and it's all going well so far.' She gave Chilcott, Fowler and Freddie a look. 'This is a first, though.'

'This has nothing do with you or your establishment, but we are interested in a couple who we think came in here on Saturday night at around 10:30 p.m.'

'Oh?' she said with a curious tone.

'We think they came here from the theatre. We believe we have them entering at…' he looked to DC Fowler for the answer.

'10:27 p.m., according to the council CCTV,' she replied without needing to look down at her notes.

'And we'd like to view them entering, staying for however long they were here, and then we are very keen to see what time they left, if that's possible, please?'

'We can certainly try to find them as they enter and leave, but I can't guarantee you'll see them inside unless they spent their time at the bar. These high booths block most camera angles when our patrons take a seat. It's part of the appeal; the privacy of my establishment.'

'Fair enough,' Chilcott said. 'Shall we see if they came in?'

'Of course. I take it you know who you're looking for?'

'Yes, shall we start at, say, 10:25 p.m. and go from there?'

The manageress typed in the date and the time, and they all stood by and watched the TV monitor. The door to the lounge bar was pictured large on the screen in full high-definition colour. They all leaned in with the same curiosity but with entirely different intentions.

The time went beyond twenty-eight minutes, and then Chilcott asked, 'Is your clock accurate on the CCTV monitor?'

'I haven't checked it for a while, I must admit.'

'Can we pause this and see what time it shows now, please?'

The manageress did as instructed. '13:44,' she said.

Chilcott checked the time on his phone.

'It's four minutes slow. Take us forward to 10:30 p.m. on Saturday night, would you, please?'

Moments later, they were watching the screen again, and at just after 10:33 p.m., the door opened outwards and in walked a female in her mid to late twenties, wearing a long brown winter coat and a bright red scarf wrapped at least once around her neck, followed closely behind by a smug-looking Travis Yardley. They waited near the door for a moment before being approached by a member of waiting staff, who then showed them to one of the high-backed booths where the female could be seen removing her coat, exposing a white low-cut blouse. Yardley kept his black leather jacket on, and they both then sank into the seat and out of sight of the camera lens.

'Do you have any other views of the entrance? Her face was turned away. We won't be able to identify her from this.'

'I'm afraid not. It's just the one camera at the door.'

Chilcott lowered his gaze. 'Who was that – the person who took them to their seats?'

'Chris,' the manageress said.

'Is Chris in now? I want to speak to him.'

'He's not on until six-thirty tonight.'

'I'll ask someone to drop by and take a quick statement from him later if that's okay with you.'

'A statement. What for?'

Chilcott leaned in closer to the screen and stared intently at the booth where Yardley and Female were hiding somewhere behind.

'I want to know what they said; what they were talking about; what their mood was; what they drank; what they ate, and most importantly, what they did.'

He looked at the manageress. 'Will that be a problem?'

'Um… you'd have to ask Chris what he remembers. We obviously see a lot of customers.'

'Do your booths have numbers?'

'Table numbers, yes.'

'And that one?'

She looked around the screen for a second. 'That looks like table eleven to me.'

'Good. Are there any other cameras located near table eleven?'

'No. Not there.'

Chilcott chomped down tightly.

'Can we fast-forward, slowly, until we see one or other of them get up from the table, please?'

'Not a problem.'

The manageress hit the x6 button, and the footage sped along like an old Benny Hill sketch complete with waiting staff whizzing briskly to and fro, and importantly, making several return trips to table eleven. And then Chilcott saw the young woman stand up from the table and walk off.

'There,' Chilcott said. 'Where's she going?'

'That's towards the ladies,' the manageress said.

They noted the time and slowed the footage down to x2 speed, and continued watching with nothing much happening for a good few minutes.

'Has she gone?' Chilcott asked impatiently.

DC Fowler and the manageress shared an exchange.

'I'd suggest they are out on a first date,' the manageress said to Chilcott.

'Why do you say that?' he said, staring at the screen.

'Body language and the fact the young lady has been in the ladies for a while. I expect she's checking her appearance, maybe running over some lines to say, or giving a detailed summary of the date to a friend.'

Chilcott looked back towards the manageress. 'You've obviously been doing this a long time?'

'Oh, yes. I'm pretty good at telling the state of a relationship before a word is ever spoken.'

Chilcott pursed his lips together. 'First date, you say?'

'Without a shadow of a doubt.'

'Okay. Let's see how this develops.' He stroked his jaw and watched as the young woman returned into the shot, her head bowed and her face just not quite clear enough to make an ID. 'Wait, they're going,' he said. 'What time are we on?'

'Eleven minutes past midnight, sir,' DC Fowler said.

'Make a note. That means that would be seven minutes past on the council footage.'

They all watched as Yardley faced the camera, holding the female's coat open for her to step inside.

'Come on,' Chilcott begged. 'Turn around. Face the camera. Show us your face.'

The female slid an arm into one sleeve of her coat, and Yardley took the opportunity to wrap her in his arms, swiftly sweeping her back and away from the camera angle.

'You twat,' Chilcott bellowed and then apologised to Pippa for his language.

And all the while, Yardley was escorting the female towards the door. He held it open with a straight arm that she ducked beneath and out into Kingsmead Square.

'Can we burn a copy of this, please?'

'Of course. It'll take me a while. Can I just check on the bar and make sure everything is okay first?'

'By all means,' Chilcott said, holding out an outstretched arm.

As the manageress left, Chilcott tapped the TV screen and whispered, 'That's our victim.'

'One of them, sir,' DC Fowler said.

'Why couldn't she turn around and face the camera?' Chilcott muttered.

'That won't be enough to go on, sir,' Fowler said.

'I know, but at least we've got Yardley, his movements and the fact he's with our victim – even if we can't identify from this footage.'

After a return to the council CCTV office, another frosty stand-off between Chilcott and the camera operator, and over an hour of Chilcott's life he was never going to see again, he was finally in receipt of some tangible lines of enquiry to progress. Yardley and the unknown female left Pippa's Lounge Bar, walked a short distance to Monmouth Place and hailed a passing taxi almost immediately. The plates were impossible to see from the Kingsmead Square CCTV camera angle. However, another camera picked up the same type of vehicle; a white Toyota Corolla Hybrid estate, driving up the Wellsway approximately five minutes later. The index number was clear to read, but the only part of the driver that could be seen was his round belly and a hand on the steering wheel. The local detective, Freddie, said the times were about right for it to be the same vehicle, and the direction of travel was consistent with a vehicle travelling away from Bath towards Hinton Charterhouse. Sadly, for Chilcott, though, that was where they lost the scent, and so the theory was hypothetical. But it was still a damn sight more than they had at the start of the day.

And now, they were standing outside of a bungalow in Twerton with the taxi parked at the front.

Chilcott rattled the glass panel of the front door with his knuckles, and they waited for a response.

The door slowly opened, and an overweight man in

tracksuit bottoms and a food-stained white T-shirt stood in the doorway.

'Yeah, what?'

'Is that your car, sir?' Chilcott asked, turning sideways so that the man could see his car at the end of the pathway.

'Who's asking, and what the fuck does it have to do with you anyway?'

Chilcott pinched his bottom lip together between his fingers and considered a *polite* response. He clicked his tongue behind his teeth and smoothed down the side of his face with a hand.

'I couldn't help but notice the lack of tread on those front tyres.'

He turned to DC Fowler. 'Detective Constable Fowler, did you notice that too? Perhaps we should call over our ever-so-friendly traffic colleagues to take a good look at the legality of that vehicle, which I also believe has a yellow taxi plate?'

'What do you want?' the man said, softening his tone.

'Is. That. Your. Vehicle, sir?'

The man considered his reply as he looked first at DC Fowler, then at the local detective and finally back to Chilcott, who was by now in no mood for dithering.

'Yeah,' he said quietly. 'What have I done?'

'You haven't done anything, sir.' Chilcott said. 'Unless you've got something you wish to get off your chest?'

The man scowled. 'I ain't done nuffin.'

'Good. Then perhaps we can talk about the reason why we're here?'

'Fuck me, that's what I—'

'I'm sorry?' Chilcott said, glancing back over his

shoulder towards the Toyota. 'You were about to say something?'

The man scowled and scratched his belly through his T-shirt.

'What? What is this?'

'Can we come inside?'

'No,' the man said, narrowing the gap in the door. 'Me misses is having a kip.'

'Fair enough. You're a private taxi driver – correct?'

The man waved a flabby arm. 'Got any ID? How do I know you lot are five-O?'

'Of course. As you asked so politely.' Three warrant badges flopped open in the man's face.

'Take your pick.'

The man pulled a face and took a half step backwards.

'So, private hire?'

'Yeah.'

'Good for you. Were you driving that vehicle on Saturday night?'

The man's eyes darted furtively between the officers and the white Toyota parked just feet away.

'This isn't about you,' Chilcott said. 'It's about someone you picked up.'

'Why didn't you say…' the man said, breathing out and visibly relaxing his shoulders.

Chilcott squinted. 'Saturday night?'

'Yeah. I was working Saturday night.'

'Until what time?'

'About four, four-thirty.'

'In the morning?'

'Yeah, of course.'

'Okay, do you keep a record of your bookings?'

'Uh… me mate will have details of any bookings.'

'And what about street pick-ups?'

'Um… Nah. We're not allowed to do street pick-ups.'

'But you did. Don't you remember?'

The man's brows met in the middle. 'How do you mean?'

'You picked up a man and a woman from near Kingsmead Square.'

The man shrugged. 'Probably picked ten couples from there through the night, but they were pre-booked.'

'Not these two. They walked out of a pub and flagged you down.'

The man scowled

'It was just past midnight. A woman in her mid to late twenties, a man a bit older.'

The man shook his head and shrugged his bulky shoulders.

'Hinton Charterhouse?'

'Uh… yeah, I did go out there.'

'Where?'

'I dunno?'

'Think.'

'Look, man, I do tonnes of drops. I can't be expected to remember all of 'em.'

Chilcott licked his tightening lips and turned to DC Fowler as he counted in multiples of a thousand silently to himself.

'Do you remember the couple?' DC Fowler asked.

'Nah.'

'How many drops did you make in Hinton Charter-house on Saturday night?'

'Dunno. Two. Three?'

Chilcott sucked up air through his nostrils like he was vacuuming the pathway.

'Think,' DC Fowler encouraged, noticing Chilcott's jaw tightening.

'I don't remember?' the man said.

'We really need to know where you dropped that couple off,' DC Fowler said calmly.

'Honestly, I—'

'Got any dash-cam?' Chilcott asked, reengaging in the conversation.

'Yeah.'

'Good. Can we have it, please?'

'Not from Saturday night, you can't. It's already wiped.'

'Jesus!' Chilcott spat through clenched teeth. 'Is it just me...?'

'Do you remember any of your customers from Saturday night?' DC Fowler persevered.

'To be honest, I don't pay much attention—'

'No shit,' Chilcott said, glaring at the man.

'How about an actor?' DC Fowler asked, doing her best to appease the taxi driver and Chilcott.

'Yeah... there was an actor.'

'Praise the Lord!' Chilcott said, looking up to the skies.

'Good,' DC Fowler said. 'Tell me about that.'

The taxi driver sniffed dismissively and scratched the fold of skin above his eyelid. 'Ain't nuffin to tell.'

'Oh, for fuck's sake. I'm going to have to go for a walk in a minute, or else I'm gonna blow.'

'Where did you take the actor?' DC Fowler asked with a professional smile.

The man shook his head. 'Dunno?'

'Could it have been Hinton Charterhouse?'

The man puffed air through a gap in the side of his mouth like he was blowing away smoke. 'Could've been?' he said.

'Look, sunshine,' Chilcott said. 'I appreciate you're never going to make it to Mensa, but we could really do with you remembering Saturday night. An actor got into your car with a woman, and you took them to Hinton Charterhouse or somewhere near there. We're not asking you to remember anything about them, what names they gave or even what they chatted about. All we need is an address, or a street, even just confirmation that you took them there.'

'Hold on…' the man said. 'The American…'

'Yes,' Chilcott quickly agreed, feeling hopeful. He watched the cogs slowly grinding in the man's head.

'Nah… still dunno?'

CHAPTER FOURTEEN

As Chilcott and DC Fowler walked briskly through the incident room towards DCI Foster's office, DC Chiba called out, 'Boss, have you got a moment, please?'

'Make it quick,' Chilcott replied, not breaking pace.

'I think you'll want to hear this, sir.'

Chilcott stopped in his tracks, and DC Fowler nearly walked right into the back of him.

'Yes. What is it, Penny? I've got to grovel to the magistrate's court for extra time. If I don't, Travis Yardley is walking out of here.'

'I followed up those enquiries with the theatre group.'

Chilcott rolled his index finger impatiently like he was winding up a long strand of wool around the finger.

'Is this story going to take an awfully long time, Penny?'

'I'll cut to the chase, sir.'

'Please do – anytime you want to start…'

'Travis Yardley was reported missing to Leicestershire police yesterday. He didn't turn up for rehearsals, and he didn't arrive for the first show last night. So, they were forced to use an understudy.'

'We know that because he's here, with us, Penny.'

'Yes, sir.'

'Is that it? I'm kind of in a hurry,' he said, starting to walk away.

'No, sir. There's more.'

Chilcott stopped himself and again wound imaginary thread around his index finger.

'I spoke to the theatre director who said that Yardley was recently acting strangely around other cast members. Several of the female cast complained of feeling *uncomfortable* around him.'

'So, he's a predator?'

'No. The director said Yardley was strange to the men as well.'

'Okay. So, he's got trouble at home, financial difficulties. He likes the bottle or a gambling habit?'

DC Chiba shook her head. 'He said it was if he was method acting, sir.'

'Method acting?' Chilcott stared. 'He's not De Niro, Penny. We're talking about a small-time jobbing actor—'

'Um…' DC Chiba said, about to correct her boss, and then thought better of it.

Chilcott left his eyes on her for a long second. 'Go on, Penny. Educate me.'

'He only started the role about three months ago, sir. He had a small background part but was also the understudy to the actor who should have been playing Jesse Garcia. That actor fell ill halfway through their five-show stint of Milton Keynes, and Travis Yardley was promoted to play Jesse

Garcia. It sounds like he didn't do very well at first, but then, in recent performances, Yardley has reportedly stolen the show. The director said it was an astonishing turn-around. Like watching a superstar in the making.'

Chilcott scratched the top of his head. 'So… he got used to the part.'

DC Chiba shook her head. 'No, sir. The director said the only way he could describe it was like Yardley *became* Jesse Garcia.'

'So, that's why he's giving us all that American bullshit with his accent. He's still acting.'

'Possibly, sir.'

Chilcott wiggled his head as he silently considered the scenario.

'Okay, so we'll tell Yardley what we now know and ask him nicely to cut the crap and behave.'

'If only crime were that simple, sir,' DC Chiba said.

'Hmm,' Chilcott mused. 'If only.'

They stood back and waited for DCI Foster to finish watching all the CCTV from Pippa's Lounge Bar and the council city centre cameras. She closed the laptop screen and turned her chair to face Chilcott, DC Fowler and DC Chiba.

'The taxi driver is a numbnuts,' Chilcott said, preempting the words about to come out of Foster's mouth. 'He can't remember a bloody thing, apart from the fact they were in his car, and the man sounded American.'

'Who is she?'

'We don't know?'

'Where did he drop them?'

'He doesn't know. And I don't think we've any chance of finding that out so long as he has a hole in his arse.'

'Thank you for your graphic prediction, Inspector Chilcott,' Foster said, looking at the other two officers with the sort of disappointing expression a parent might use for a wayward child. 'Perhaps just stick to the facts, would you.'

'Penny has done some good work around the theatre contacts,' Chilcott said. 'Yardley was an understudy who was recently promoted to the role of Jesse Garcia. And by all accounts, he was crap at first but is now a rising star in the making.'

'So, what changed?'

'We don't know yet, but I can't wait to ask him.'

'Ma'am,' DC Chiba said.

'Yes, Penny.'

'The theatre director said he was acting strangely around the other cast members. They could tell something wasn't right with him.'

'But he was turning in good performances?'

Chilcott cut over DC Chiba before she could answer. 'That's what they say, though, don't they? It's like your favourite comedians are tortured, miserable bastards when they're not performing. I remember seeing—'

'Yes – thank you again, Robbie,' DCI Foster glared.

'Okay,' she said, collecting her thoughts. 'So, we need to find out who this female is? The custody clock is rapidly running down, and I don't want us to be forced to release Travis Yardley because we haven't found her.'

'That's about the size of it.'

'Any thoughts?'

'I'm going to sit down with Yardley and turn the screw, see what cracks,' Chilcott said.

'What if he doesn't?' DCI Foster said.

Chilcott pouted. 'We know stuff now that we didn't know before. He can't keep the act going all night.'

'Or maybe he can.'

'He's got to start playing ball sooner or later.'

'I want us to put out a press release as soon as possible. I want you to go back to Hinton Charterhouse and speak to the media. I'll contact the press officer and arrange for the cameras to meet you there.'

'Hold on…'

'We need to find this female, and we need to find her fast. I'm not prepared to release those poor close-up images of her now, but let's share a far-off view of them getting into the taxi at the end of the night. It might be enough to trigger a memory, or perhaps someone might recognise the female's clothing and put two and two together if they haven't spoken to her for a day or two?'

'What about his interview?'

'That can wait. We're finally building a case. Let's not lose impetus.'

'What about Yardley. Do we release his name to the press?'

Foster studied Chilcott's face for a moment.

'Yes. It's a fact that he is helping us with our investigation.'

'It could ruin his career, Ma'am. Guilty or not,' DC Fowler offered.

'It probably will. We know how the media will shred

every last sinew out of the story. But maybe, just maybe, that could also help us.'

DC Fowler dropped her head.

'Amy, I don't think any of us are in doubt that he has done something he shouldn't. That female is out there somewhere, and we need to find her and fast. We can then compare her DNA to the blood found on Yardley's body.'

DC Fowler continued looking down at her feet. 'I just know how the press will feed on this, Ma'am. It's a shame if he's innocent.'

'Nature of the beast, I'm afraid, kiddo,' Chilcott said.

'In fact,' DCI Fowler said. 'Amy's got a point. Innocent until proven guilty and all that, but let's interview him again – tell him we will release his name to the national press unless he starts cooperating. Let's bluff him, see how he responds? That should be enough incentive for him to drop the ridiculous act and start telling us what really happened.'

'And if he doesn't?' Chilcott said.

'If he doesn't… we'll have no choice but to feed him to the sharks.'

CHAPTER FIFTEEN

The duty solicitor had an hour in private consultation with Travis Yardley. Now, they were once again the width of a table from one another. This time, Chilcott was in a determined mood, and Yardley was still not appearing to give a damn about his precarious position.

'We know you're an actor,' Chilcott said, slowly running the tips of his fingers across his brow. He continued staring down at the table. It wasn't a comment for debate. It was a nailed-on fact.

'We know your real name is Travis Yardley. We also know that Jesse Garcia is a fictional character who you play in a stage show.'

DC Fowler slid an A4 colour photo of Yardley, taken from his acting website.

'Look at it,' she said.

Yardley sneered as he picked up the sheet of paper and spent a few seconds admiring the image of himself.

'I've just come back from obtaining extra custody time from the magistrates,' Chilcott said. 'You're not going anywhere, sunshine. We can legally keep you here for another forty-eight hours. That's mid-afternoon Thursday.'

Mr Wilson gave Chilcott a lingering look. Forty-eight hours wasn't the maximum time Chilcott could have obtained. He could have been given a further thirty-six hours. That meant the magistrates didn't have absolute confidence in the police case. Chilcott already knew that, and now, so did Mr Wilson.

'Why don't we start again, Mr Yardley? Please give us your full name, date of birth and current home address,' she said

Yardley placed the photoprint back down onto the table and straightened it up so that it was neatly positioned in front of him.

DC Fowler waited.

'I am Jesse Garcia. Born July sixteen, nineteen seventy-seven. I live in Miami, Florida, USA.' As he spoke, he maintained his southern US accent.

DC Fowler looked up to the camera recording the conversation.

'We know that is incorrect, Mr Yardley. We know that you are an English actor and you have been playing the character role of Jesse Garcia on stage. We also know that you were born Elliott John Coates in Coventry, England on the fifth of November nineteen eighty-three and that Travis Yardley is your public persona.'

Yardley dismissed the claim with a *pfft*, and looked at Kevin Wilson, who casually waved an unconcerned hand but said nothing.

'Can I have that other document, please?' Chilcott asked DC Fowler.

She handed Chilcott another A4-sized printed document.

'You would have seen this before, many times, I'm guessing,' he said, laying the document face-up on the desk. 'This is your actor profile taken from the website. We can see your headshot, and your personal details, as have just been set out by my colleague. And, we can see your acting history and the roles you've taken.'

He pushed the sheet in front of Yardley and steepled his fingers, watching his subject read the information from the sheet of paper.

'Shall we do away with the dramatics now and have a serious conversation about how you came to be smeared in the blood of two different people.'

Yardley pushed the document back in Chilcott's direction. 'I can't help you there.'

Chilcott pointed a rigid finger towards Yardley's face.

'Right, for starters, let's do away with this ridiculous accent, shall we.'

'I beg your pardon?' Yardley said.

'Please speak in your native English tongue.'

Yardley frowned and looked again at Mr Wilson.

'Uh…' Wilson uttered.

'I've watched several interviews of you on the internet today, and you most certainly did not have an American accent in any of them,' DC Fowler said.

Yardley slid his eyes sideways towards DC Fowler.

'Enough,' Chilcott glared. 'Mr Wilson, would you like to speak to your client before we continue with this interview further?'

'Honestly, I don't think there's much I can say over and

above the advice I've already provided my client. I'd also like to comment that I see no issues whatsoever with the current line of questioning.'

Yardley gave his brief a long, measured stare.

'Mr Yardley, tell us everything you know about the blood on your body in the early hours of Sunday the sixth of March this year,' Chilcott asked.

'Hmmm,' Yardley purred as if with self-satisfaction.

'Explain how you came to be in the middle of nowhere on the B3110 wearing only boxer shorts.'

Yardley took a finger and began routing it around the inside of his nose.

Chilcott slid forwards on his elbows, reducing the gap between himself and Yardley. It was a subtle display of dominance.

'At approximately ten twenty-one hours on Saturday the fifth of March, you were seen leaving the side entrance of the Theatre Royal, Bath with a female. Who is she?'

Yardley closed his eyes and deliberately sucked air in through his nose. He blew it back out into Chilcott's face with an 'ahhhh.' His face brightened. 'Delightful.'

'Where is that person now?'

Yardley stroked the back of his head, but didn't answer.

'You are being investigated for the murder of two persons who at this time remain unidentified. It could significantly aid your situation if you tell us everything you know about these suspected murders.'

When Yardley didn't speak, Chilcott looked to Mr Wilson, who shrugged a resigned shoulder.

'We are going to make your name public unless you

cooperate. Do you have any idea what that will do to your career?'

'Uh, I'm not sure of the legal stance with that stunt, Detective Inspector,' Mr Wilson countered.

'It's not a stunt, Mr Wilson. We have identified a suspect in a grave crime, and disclosing his name and image has a significant chance of assisting members of the public in coming forward with information that will aid the police in their investigation. In the absence of Mr Yardley providing any such information, we are left with little option.' Chilcott looked across the table and held Yardley's heavy stare.

'Can I have a private moment with my client, please?' Mr Wilson asked.

'I wish you would,' Chilcott said and paused the interview, leaving the room with DC Fowler.

'Here, we go,' Chilcott said quietly to DC Fowler outside the interview room door. 'That should do the trick. It's time to find our victims.'

The door to the interview room opened, and Kevin Wilson stuck his head out into the corridor.

'Sorry,' he said. 'But we're not changing our position or our accent. I'm sorry, Robbie.'

Chilcott acknowledged him with a head bob and followed Mr Wilson back into the room.

He re-took his seat opposite Yardley and steepled his hands in front of his face. He observed Yardley menacingly from above the dome of his knuckles.

'We know that you and a female took a taxi from Kingsmead Square a little over two hours before you were found covered in blood.' Suddenly, Chilcott slammed both hands down on the table, creating a loud bang and making DC Fowler and Mr Wilson jump. But not Yardley.

'Tell us where she is, you piece of shit,' Chilcott boomed.

'U… uh…' the duty solicitor stammered. 'I don't think you should—'

'I said tell us where she is,' Chilcott seethed through gritted teeth.

Yardley's face cracked into a smile, and he looked at his solicitor. 'Is this guy for real?'

Chilcott felt a furnace of anger welling deep within him. He balled his fists and panted deeply through his nostrils.

'Um… if I may?' Mr Wilson said, looking down at Chilcott's clenched fists. 'Perhaps, I may speak with my client again?'

'No, you may not,' Chilcott snapped back, not taking his eyes from his suspect.

'I'm sorry, but you can't dictate—'

'Where is she?' Chilcott said through gritted teeth, and over the top of an increasingly-flustered duty solicitor.

Yardley smiled with his broad *Hollywood* grin.

'It's your last chance to tell us.'

'My client is reserving his legal rights not to answer your questions,' Mr Wilson said in a frosty, defensive tone.

'Don't say we didn't warn you,' Chilcott seethed. He lifted his shirt sleeve and looked long and hard at his wristwatch.

'Less than two hours from now, I'm speaking to the national media. I'm releasing your name and telling them you are assisting police with an ongoing murder inquiry.'

The solicitor jerked his head back and sat up bolt rigid. 'You're doing what?'

'There's only one way to stop me from doing that, son. Tell me where she is.'

'Fuck you,' Yardley scoffed.

Chilcott sprang up from his seat and stormed for the door. He stopped at the exit and turned with an outstretched, pointed finger. 'No. Fuck you.'

'I think you need to take a global view of this,' Foster said as Chilcott prowled like a menacing lion inside the DCI's office.

'I don't give a shit if he never acts a day of his life again,' Chilcott spewed. 'Just get me to those cameras. I'm going to piss on his parade.'

'You need to calm down. Take a step back and calm down.'

Chilcott clamped his jaw and looked wildly at his boss.

'I've asked Jaz to go with you to the press release,' she said. 'If you lose your head to the cameras, it won't do anyone any good. Not least, our victims.'

'I haven't got time to brief Chowdhury with the details.'

'I've already done it. He's an expert at handling the media, remember. He knows all the right things to say.'

'I just don't get this act – why is he still pursuing it? It's not doing him any good.'

'I suspect he's had a mental episode of some kind. The pressure. The stress of touring. Who knows?'

Chilcott stared vacantly into space, his chest still heaving with frustration.

'What is it?' Foster asked him.

'We need to concentrate on finding the female. We're getting distracted by his act – what if that is part of his ploy? I just can't understand why we haven't found her. Hinton Charterhouse is a tiny village, and we've done the house-to-house—'

'But we didn't get responses everywhere.'

'No. But being a small village, people will talk. It's only natural and only a matter of time before someone notices that something is amiss.'

'Maybe we need to focus on a wider area?'

'There's nothing else there – just roads leading to the next villages, several kilometres away. I don't believe he walked that far. Someone would surely have spotted him walking the roads at night in his state of undress?'

'That's why we're putting it out to the media, isn't it?'

Chilcott rolled his neck. His shoulders were beginning to stiffen. 'I guess.'

'This isn't about you versus Yardley, Robbie. I get your frustration; I really do. But we must stay focussed on finding that female.'

Chilcott left his eyes on the DCI. 'Trust me. I'm not resting until we've found her.'

CHAPTER SIXTEEN

Jaz Chowdhury had made significant progress with the media press release, and the DCI had organised a special live statement to the cameras at 6:05 p.m. Chowdhury would deliver the official statement. Chilcott would be on hand to field any tricky questions should they arise. Given the scarcity of evidence so far, Chilcott anticipated being the busier of the two inspectors.

They planned to hold the press release in the Fox and Hounds car park in Hinton Charterhouse. This had three main advantages; firstly, it gave the general public the message that the police were in the community dealing with the problem. Secondly, it might trigger the memory of someone who may have driven through the village and seen the American walking along the road but not called it in for whatever reason. And thirdly, the car park was large enough to cater for the various mobile broadcast units that would swoop down like locusts at a cornfield at chow time.

Chowdhury rehearsed the opening lines repeatedly as they drove towards the small village. So much so Chilcott was getting irritated by the nuanced emphasis he was putting on certain words.

'I think you know it by now,' Chilcott said, gripping the wheel a little tighter.

'You only have one chance to get it right to the cameras, Robbie.'

'I'll bet you a tenner you fluff it.'

Chowdhury stopped rehearsing and stared at his colleague.

'I can't believe you just said that.'

'Just saying – too much practice leads to errors.'

'On the contrary. If I get the first lines out without a hitch, the rest will follow. Have you never followed a script?'

'Funnily enough… no.'

'You leave the press release to me, and I'll leave answering the tricky questions to you.'

'Gee, thanks. You're all heart.'

As they exited the blackness of the countryside and entered the sporadic streetlights of Hinton Charterhouse, Chilcott drew in several long, slow breaths as his heart rate quickened.

'What time are we on now?' Chilcott asked, even though he could see the time on the dashboard.

'Coming up on six o'clock.'

As they rounded the left-hand bend towards the main four-way junction at the centre of the village, Chilcott saw the bright arc of mobile floodlights illuminating the clear night sky above the pub car park.

'Looks like they're ready for us,' he said.

'I need to practise a couple more times before we—'

'Don't worry, Jaz. We said five past six, so five past six it will be.'

Chilcott slowed the unmarked Ford Mondeo, indicated off the main road and turned up the slight incline into the large pub car park. Unlike the last time when his was the only vehicle in the thirty or so spaced car park, this time, he was forced to park in an overflow waste ground at the back.

'Ready for this,' Chilcott said, killing the headlights and ignition.

'Always.'

Chilcott cast a sideways glance at his confident colleague, and in the corner of his eye, he saw a maelstrom of reporters coming their way.

'Break a leg,' he said and winked.

'Ha – very good. It looks like the vultures are ready to feed.'

Chilcott turned back to look through the windscreen, and bright lights dazzled his eyes.

'C'mon then. Let's throw them some bones.'

The two DIs stepped out of the car and wrapped their overcoats tighter around their bodies. The chill air was barely above freezing, and the rising condensation from the gaggle of press officers, camera operators and hot lamps created a rising steam cloud much like scrum time at a rugby match.

Chilcott took a moment to wrap a scarf around his neck and pulled on some black insulated gloves as the reporters scrambled to be the first to reach the officers.

Chilcott held out his gloved hands in front of him to temper their eagerness.

'Calm down. Calm down. Give us a chance to get out of the car, will you.'

'What can you tell us about the investigation?' an unknown and impatient female voice came from the front of the silhouetted gaggle.

Chilcott looked down at his watch even though he could barely see the face hands in the dark.

'Shall we go back over there,' he suggested, making the reporters turn and stumble over one another to get the prime position.

He looked at the broadcast vans parked around the extremities of the pub car park, huge satellite dishes pointing northwards. Sky. ITN. BBC and a couple of others that didn't wear their logos with quite the same pride or price tag. He was surprised at the auspicious turnout. Just what had the press office told them?

'Here will do,' he said, making a point not to have the pub name or entrance in the shot. It might have been good publicity for the small village hostelry, but it wasn't appropriate to have their name associated with a crime they had nothing to do with.

After a bit more jostling and fighting for prime real estate by the visiting crews, Chilcott and Chowdhury stood shoulder to shoulder in the glare of the halogen lights.

Chilcott recognised the regional ITN reporter, Stella Murphy, at the end of the front row. She had been doing this gig for as long as he had, and she was as good as gold to deal with, unlike some of the newshounds who would try every sneaky trick in the book to get exclusive material from the slightest slip of the tongue or ill-conceived remark. He didn't recognise the other reporters and assumed they had travelled from somewhere other than the Bristol news hub.

Chilcott nudged his colleague in the side with mere moments to go until the live feed and with the reporters practicing their patter to the camera operators for one last time.

'Okay, Jaz. Are you good to go, mate?'

'I am. I don't fancy your chances much, though. They look hungry.'

'Just remember, you could be the face of breakfast TV by morning.'

'As if I needed any more pressure.'

Chilcott then noticed Stella Murphy attempting to get his attention and tapping the face of her watch. He checked his watch against the shaft of light from the press floodlights.

It's showtime.

Chowdhury gave Chilcott a withering look and then stepped slightly forwards into the waiting lenses.

'In the early hours of Sunday morning,' Chowdhury confidently began, 'a male was located not far from where we stand tonight. He was walking along the main B3110 between Hinton Charterhouse and Midford, near Bath. He was semi-naked, wearing only boxer shorts, and he was smeared in a considerable amount of what we have now confirmed to be blood. A paramedic crew initially picked him up after a passing motorist called emergency services to his location. As a result, the male was taken to the Royal United Hospital, where a thorough examination revealed that he had not suffered any personal injury. The police were notified, promptly attended the hospital and swiftly secured evidence. Officers visiting the scene, where the male was located at the roadside, have failed to identify the source of blood found upon the male. Following medical discharge from the hospital, the male was conveyed to Keynsham Police Detention Centre, where he remains assisting detectives with ongoing enquiries. We do not wish to alarm the general public. However, at this time, little is known about how the male came to be covered with blood. We would ask that any persons who may have seen this gentleman either on the B3110 or elsewhere, at a time estimated between 1:30 and 2 a.m. on Sunday morning, come forward and provide detectives with as much information as possible. No matter how insignificant you may consider it to be. At this time, officers are working diligently to secure evidence in these unusual circumstances. If you are aware of someone who lives in the Hinton Charterhouse area, who has not arrived for work since the weekend. Or hasn't responded to calls, texts or social media since the early hours of Sunday morning. I would encourage you to contact the control room on 101, or phone anonymously via Crime Stoppers. We must identify and exclude as many local residents from our enquiries as soon as possible. Detective Inspector Chilcott is the deputy senior investigating officer and will now take a limited number of questions. Thank you.'

'Would it be fair to say that you suspect foul play, hence the reason you are holding this press conference?' the SKY reporter asked, making sure he got in before the others.

Chilcott gave Chowdhury a wary glance and stepped in the bright spot vacated by his now, visibly-relieved colleague, who was slowly slinking away into the shadows.

'Thank you for the question,' Chilcott said. 'We are keeping an open mind at this time. We have no firm evidence that a crime of any kind has been committed.'

'But you wouldn't be standing here in the cold if you thought no crime had been committed,' the SKY reporter persisted.

'We are here to raise public awareness of this matter in the hope that the great British public provides us with any information that could help progress this inquiry further.'

'So, what you're saying is you are basically out of ideas.'

Chilcott locked eyes with the reporter.

'Any other constructive questions?' he said, turning to the other reporters.

'Hello, Detective Chilcott – Stella Murphy, ITN.'

'Hello, Miss Murphy. Please, go ahead.'

'Is the male communicating with police?' she asked.

'Communication has been limited, particularly relating to the circumstances surrounding his location, attire and the presence of blood upon his person.'

'Is there a reason for his lack of cooperation?'

Chilcott rocked slightly on his heels. 'That is what we need to establish.'

'Has the male provided a name?' the SKY reporter cut back in.

'He has. However, we have reason to believe that the furnished details are… inaccurate.'

'Inaccurate in what way?' the reporter persisted.

Chilcott fixed his gaze upon the young reporter. 'They aren't correct,' he said in a deliberately patronising way.

'What can you tell us about the blood?' the BBC reporter asked doggedly.

Chilcott brought a hand to his mouth and quietly cleared his throat. The second he did it, he realised his body language betrayed the truth he knew.

'Nothing at this time,' he said quickly.

'But you've analysed it. Can you confirm or deny if it is human blood?'

'We are not in a position to make any rash statements until we have more information – which is why we are reaching out to the good people of this area at this time.'

'Are you suspecting murder, Detective Inspector Chilcott?' the reporter with the irritating voice asked.

'We are keeping an open mind to every eventuality.'

'So, police aren't ruling it out?'

Chilcott leaned forwards. 'It would be foolish to rule out any eventuality at this embryonic stage of an investigation.'

Several of the reporters spoke over one another at once, but the unknown female reporter's voice was the one that penetrated Chilcott's ears.

'Is it right that you have British actor Travis Yardley in your custody, Inspector?'

The hubbub from all the reporters ended in that split-second. And Chilcott felt a weight of expectation descend upon his shoulders.

'I'm not in a position to divulge—'

'Our sources have confirmed that you have Travis Yardley in your custody. Will you confirm that the semi-naked male you have detained and Travis Yardley are the same people?'

Chilcott blinked and instinctively turned for Chowd-hury's support, only too aware he was on live television. He wanted to grab the reporter and tell her to stick her camera where the sun doesn't shine, but instead, he did his best to maintain a professional exterior.

'Thank you. That is all,' he said and turned away from the cameras, noticing Chowdhury had already moved back several paces.

'Rather you than me,' Chowdhury said as Chilcott passed him on his way to the Mondeo.

'I messed up. I let that upstart get to me.'

'You sounded great. It's good to see the human side of policing at this type of media release. The public connects better with emotion.'

Chilcott checked his stride and glanced at his colleague.

'Was I that bad?'

'Not *that* bad.'

Chowdhury grinned. 'I'm pulling your leg.'

'I'm not so sure. Anything from the incident room?'

'Nothing yet.'

'Come on, Jaz. I need a sugar hit and something warm inside me. I owe you a tenner; the hot chocolates are on me.'

CHAPTER SEVENTEEN

They waved goodbye to the reporters, some of whom were still giving their analysis of the press conference to live camera feeds, and entered the bar of the Fox and Hounds.

It was quiet; actually, it was just the two of them, plus two bar staff and a local man who seemed to be welded to a stool at the bar. They took two comfy armchair seats beside the open fire and rubbed warmth back into their hands as they waited for their drinks. They were far enough away from the bar area to be unheard but close enough to listen in should anything interesting come their way.

'Didn't I just see you two on the TV?' the barman said as he delivered the hot drinks – complete with a tower of whipped cream, dark chocolate buttons and a dusting of cocoa powder that appeared to go everywhere but on the top of the drinks.

'That's right,' Chilcott replied, wondering why the barman hadn't gone the whole hog and stuck a cocktail brolly in the drinks. 'We were reporting on the unusual incident from the other night.'

'Yeah,' the barman said, looking off distantly and spilling some of Chowdhury's drink on the saucer and table in the process. 'He's a strange bugger in-ee?' the old boy said.

'That's fine, don't worry,' Chowdhury said, anticipating an apology and possibly a serviette, neither of which materialised.

'So, what do you think about it then?' Chilcott asked the old barman. It wasn't a spontaneous decision bringing Chowdhury here, and he was secretly delighted to have a bite already.

'Bloody foreigners.'

'I beg your pardon?' Chowdhury said, sitting upright in his chair.

The barman looked at Chowdhury and Chilcott and postured dismissively.

'Not you. Them lot from London.'

Chilcott looked at his colleague and subtly shook his head before engaging the man again.

'Would you happen to know if there is a family of Londoners living nearby?'

'No. Why, should I?'

'My apologies, it's just the way you said—'

'Don't know why they have to come 'ere with their fancy cars and money.'

'Have you lived in Hinton Charterhouse long?' Chilcott said.

'Seventy-one years, man and boy. I grew up where that convenience store is now. Bloody shame what they did to that place.'

'And what about this lovely place – how long have you worked here?'

'Came 'ere first during the Falklands War in eighty-two.' The barman's eyes glazed as he stared away distantly. 'Bloody shame all that business, why we had to go to war—'

'Is Bill bothering you with his war stories, gentlemen?'

Chilcott looked behind. It was Sandra, the publican.

'He's certainly keeping us entertained.'

'Go on, Bill,' Sandra said. 'I heard the door go; we have customers to serve.'

Bill emitted a frustrated, low-pitched groan and shuffled away from the table.

'Sorry about Bill,' Sandra said.

'Salt of the earth,' Chilcott said, watching the old boy walk behind the high countertop and through a doorway and out of sight. 'Not too genned up on political correctness, but salt of the earth nonetheless. So…' Chilcott said, leaning in closer towards Sandra, which in turn caused her to hinge forwards as if they were sharing a juicy secret. 'Any gossip or theories come your way from the locals since we last spoke?'

'No, nothing. It's like it never happened. All this, though…' she gestured out of the large plate-glass windows towards the car park. 'The tongues will be wagging tonight with all this attention.'

'I didn't ask you before, but are you aware of any unusual cult groups or practices taking place around here?'

'What like pagan witchcraft and such?'

'It could be one theory?'

'Nah, that's all nonsense. Nothing like that around here. This is a good Christian community.'

'Are there many churchgoers in Hinton, do you know?'

'There are a few die-hards, I suppose.'

'Who is the local vicar?'

'We share Reverend Jarvis with neighbouring villages within the parish, but he's here most Sundays.'

Chilcott pouted. 'That's good to know. Is there a contact number somewhere for Reverend Jarvis?'

'On the website, I expect.'

'Of course.'

At that, the doors opened and in walked the unknown and annoying news reporter, complete with a vibrant-red knitted scarf and matching bobble hat and gloves.

'I thought I saw you both come in here,' she called out from across the room.

'Thanks,' Chilcott said to Sandra, ignoring the reporter. 'Do me a favour,' he whispered to Sandra. 'Don't say too much to the reporters, okay?'

'Right you are,' she replied and returned behind the counter with barely a glance at the oncoming journalist.

'We haven't met before this evening. I'm Taylor Walker,' the reporter said, bounding over towards Chilcott and Chowdhury. She placed an outstretched hand between them both.

Chowdhury was the first to accept it.

'Good evening, Miss Walker,' he said.

'That was some interview,' Chilcott said, waiting his turn to shake the young woman's hand.

'It's some story,' she replied smugly.

Chilcott curled a lip. 'Hmmm. To some, maybe.'

'So, come on, off the record,' she said, dragging over a

stool to sit alongside Chowdhury. 'What do you think has happened?'

'I'm not sure you lot know the meaning of "off the record", do you?'

'Don't be like that.'

'Do I detect an accent?' Chilcott mused.

'East Sussex,' she said proudly.

'Brighton?'

'Bexhill.'

'Never been there myself.'

'I know what you're trying to do,' she smiled. 'I wasn't born yesterday.'

'I'd hope not.'

'Come on – off the record. What has Travis Yardley done?'

Chilcott looked first over his left shoulder and then over his right. He wiggled his index finger towards the reporter and leaned in closer. 'Off the record,' he said quietly. 'Watch the news, and you may find out.'

The reporter laughed arrogantly and looked around, just as Chilcott had done. 'Well,' she said. 'I'm sure the locals will have plenty to say on the matter, even if the police don't.'

'Why let the truth get in the way of a good story?' Chowdhury said.

'Do you know what? It's amazing how many police officers say that – usually when they're absolutely clueless about what they're doing.'

'I'm intrigued,' Chilcott said. 'Where did you get the information regarding Travis Yardley being in police cells?'

'So, it's true. He is with you?'

'I didn't say that. I asked you where you got the information from?'

'I'm not going to divulge the details of my contacts.' She smiled with the sort of expression that was somewhere between complacency and suffering a bad case of flatulence.

'Then I'm not going to divulge sensitive police information,' Chilcott said.

'You have already.'

Chilcott's leg was *ticking* under the table. 'Come on,' he said to Chowdhury. 'Let's get back to the office. This hot chocolate suddenly tastes bitter.'

As they walked away, Chilcott stopped and turned back.

'Have you met Bill?' he said, placing an arm on Bill's shoulder.

'Not yet, but I intend to,' the reporter replied.

'Perhaps you could tell Bill all about where you hail from. He loves to hear from Londoners.'

'I am *not* a Londoner.'

Chilcott turned to the old barman. 'She's all yours, Bill. Don't hold back, my friend.'

'Bloody hell,' Bill grumbled, tightening his grip around a dishcloth in his hands.

Chilcott looked back and extended the reporter a two-finger salute as they left through the large double swing doors.

CHAPTER EIGHTEEN

It took them almost fifty minutes to arrive back at the incident room. Chilcott had stewed the whole way back, and Chowdhury knew better than to interrupt Chilcott when he was deep in thought.

'Any update?' Chilcott asked as they strode purposefully through the incident room. A team of five detectives had the sole purpose of fielding incoming calls resulting from the press release, like a mini Crimewatch call centre.

'It's been a pretty good response, boss,' DC McEwan said. 'A couple of drivers saying they think they saw him on the roadside but didn't stop.'

'Where exactly?'

'The main B3110, boss.'

'That doesn't take us any further. We already know that.'

'We've also had the usual nut-job calls, too; alien abductions, Elvis and the like.'

'Is there anything worth following up tonight?'

McEwan rocked his head. 'Not from me, boss. I don't know about the others?'

A hand went up from DC Penny Chiba on the opposite side of the desk, and she beckoned Chilcott and Chowdhury over to her. She was talking on the phone.

'Mrs Coates,' she said, 'would you mind if I just put you on hold for a second, please?'

DC Chiba pressed the mute button and turned to Chilcott and Chowdhury with lively, wide-eyed excitement.

'I've got his ex-wife on the line,' she whispered, even though the line was muted.

'Where is she?'

'She's in St Albans, North of London, sir.'

'What's she saying?'

'I've only been talking to her for about half a minute, sir. She saw the TV report and heard her husband's name.'

'Can I?' Chilcott asked, holding out a hand to take the phone receiver.

DC Chiba vacated her chair, and Chilcott sat down. *Mrs Coates?* he mouthed to DC Chiba, who nodded.

'Hello, Mrs Coates. My name is Detective Inspector Robbie Chilcott.'

'Oh, hello,' Mrs Coates answered, sounding anxious.

'I don't know if my colleague has already told you, but the investigation team are based in Bristol.'

'Um, yes. Yes, she did say something about that.'

'And is it right that you are in St Albans?'

'Yes. Nearby. I'm with my parents.'

'Visiting?'

'No, I… I live here… now.' Her voice trailed away.

'Can I ask the reason for you calling the incident room tonight, please? I don't want to make any assumptions.'

'I heard my ex-husband's name mentioned on the TV. Was it you? Were you the one on the TV?'

'Yes, it was me. I'm very sorry you heard about your husband this way.'

'Is it true? Has Travis been arrested?'

Chilcott glanced up at the others watching him keenly.

'Yes. I'm afraid to say that Travis Yardley has been arrested. And he is helping us with our investigation.'

'Investigation? What has he done?' Mrs Coates' voice was wavering as she spoke.

'We… we don't yet know, to be honest, Mrs Coates.'

'Then why has he been arrested?'

'Mrs Coates, your husb— sorry, ex-husband is fine. He's in one of our police stations near Bath.'

Mrs Coates didn't respond.

'Has Travis had anything significant happen to him recently, perhaps, something that might have bothered him unduly – money worries, a difficult family bereavement…?'

Mrs Coates went quiet for half a minute as she thought about the question.

'I can only think about his latest job. It was causing him quite a lot of anxiety. He was forced to stand in for one of the lead roles at short notice.'

'Jesse Garcia?'

'Yes. He wasn't receiving very good reviews and was beating himself up over it. I told him not to read the reviews, but he still did.'

'How often do you see him, Mrs Coates?'

'We talk every weekend. He calls to speak with Amelia and Lily-Belle.'

'Amelia and Lily-Belle – your daughters?'

'Yes, our daughters. We may be separated, but that doesn't mean our daughters have to suffer too. They love him dearly.'

Chilcott glanced up at the others again.

'And did he call you over the weekend?'

'Yes, he did. He sounded really positive. He said the recent shows were amazing. He said everyone was raving—'

'Was that Saturday?'

'Yes.'

'Just gone?'

'Yes.'

'What time?'

'It was around 3 p.m., I think?'

'This might sound an odd question, but what accent was he using?'

'His accent, of course.'

'English?'

'Yes?' Mrs Coates' tone had turned questioning.

'How long did you speak for?'

'I chatted with him briefly, and then he face-timed Amelia and Lily-Belle for nearly half an hour.'

'In his English accent?'

'Yes… look, what's this about?'

'Has your ex-husband ever suffered from schizophrenia?'

'What? No. Of course not. Why would you ask that?'

'Because he is displaying some unusual behaviour, Mrs Coates.'

'Yes, you've already said that, but what do you mean?'

Mrs Coates sounded increasingly concerned.

'The hospital doctors assessed Travis, and they said he

displayed no signs of psychological or physical trauma. But we need to understand why he's acting the way he is.'

'Acting how? I'm sorry, I really don't know what you are talking about? It doesn't sound like Trav at all. He's never been in trouble with the police.'

Chilcott raised a brow. 'You said he was getting anxious about the role he was playing. Why was that an issue for this show in particular?'

'It was his first really big part, and he was desperate to get it right. He said it could be the springboard for a career into films.'

'How did that anxiety display itself to you?'

'Well, Trav is a very kind and gentle man. But his character in the play is controlling and evil and really at odds with Trav's own passive nature. So, that conflict created quite an issue for him.'

'But he's an actor. That's what they do, is it not?'

'Yes, I suppose so.'

'Has he played that type of character before?'

'No, I don't think so, and he certainly hasn't had a stage role quite as big as this before.'

'Has he ever slipped into character when he's been with you or talking to you over the phone?'

'No, but he's really fantastic at taking off accents. I think that was one of the reasons he got this role.'

'Because of his ability to speak in an American accent?'

'Yes. He makes impressions too.' She giggled nervously. 'He can mimic pretty much anyone once he's heard them speak for a while.

'That's interesting. Thank you for being so candid.'

There was a silence for a beat, and then Mrs Coates asked, 'Is Trav in trouble?'

Chilcott bit down his top lip and sighed. 'I'm afraid so. Your husband was found walking on a country road outside of Bath in the small hours of Sunday morning. He was smeared in a significant amount of blood—'

'Oh, God! Is he okay?'

'He's fine. He's absolutely fine. But our concern is where this blood came from and how it came to be on your husband's body.'

Mrs Coates fell deathly silent.

'Mrs Coates, this is the early stages of the investigation, and I'm going be honest, I have no idea which direction this is headed. However, your ex-husband isn't cooperating with us in any way at all.'

'What?' she breathed. 'Why not?'

'That's what we'd all like to know.'

Chilcott could hear Mrs Coates sobbing in the receiver.

'Mrs Coates, are your parents with you?'

'Yes,' she replied softly.

'Just bear with me a moment. I'm going to put the phone on hold.'

Chilcott hit the mute button and quickly typed something into a search browser.

'Mrs Coates, I have an idea that might help your ex-husband and all of us in the process.'

'Y... yes'

'If I get you a return train ticket and a hotel room, would you agree to come to Bristol to see your ex-husband?'

'I... I'd have to...'

'If we said tomorrow – could you come? I've just

checked, and it takes two and half hours by train. You won't have to pay for a thing. All transport and accommodation will be on us.'

'I'd have to make arrangements for the school.'

'It could really help your ex-husband's case.'

'You would let me see him?'

'Yes. You won't be allowed to talk about the case, but if he sees a familiar face, then perhaps it could help?'

'Of course, I'd like to help him if I can, but…'

'I can arrange for a police car to drop you a rail warrant tonight to allow you to get down to Bristol tomorrow.'

'Honestly, no. There's no need for that. I can make my own way to Bristol. I'll get there as soon as I can. I'll do anything to help Travis.'

'Leave it with me, I'll pull some strings, and perhaps I can authorise a Premier Inn or something like that for a couple of days. You won't have to go to any expense. I believe your presence here will help us out immensely.'

'Okay,' Mrs Coates whispered.

'Good night, Mrs Coates. I look forward to seeing you tomorrow morning.'

CHAPTER NINETEEN

Wednesday 9th March

11:16 a.m.

Mrs Coates sat perched on the lip of a soft chair in the DCI's office, her hands clutching her knees. Chilcott and Foster were making small-talk, trying their best to put their guest at ease. Mrs Coates was an attractive woman – very attractive – with the kind of radiant blue eyes that could halt conversations when she walked into a room. Only now, they were sunken pools of anguish and pain. Aged somewhere in her mid-thirties, she and Travis Yardley indeed made for a handsome couple.

'So, how was your journey?' Chilcott asked her breezily.

'Fine. It was fine. Thank you.'

Mrs Coates didn't know where to look, so she spent most

of the time looking down at the space just in front of her knees.

'I'm sure this is all quite surreal for you,' DCI Foster said.

'I've never been inside a police station before,' Mrs Coates blushed.

'Well, technically, this isn't a police station in the traditional sense of the word. We don't have marked police vehicles responding to ongoing incidents from here. This building houses specialist units, such as major crime, which is what we do,' she said, gesturing to Chilcott to include him in the conversation.

'Major crime?'

'That's right.'

'Like murders and things?'

'Like murders and things,' Chilcott repeated.

Mrs Coates' shoulders tightened. She moved her bottom closer to the edge of the seat. 'I don't understand?' she said with desperate eyes looking for answers between Chilcott and Foster.

'Can we get you a drink of anything? A tea or coffee, perhaps?' DCI Foster asked.

Mrs Coates shook her head. 'I just want to see my ex-husband,' she said timidly.

'Your ex-husband isn't in this building,' Foster said. 'We wanted to talk to you first before you see him.'

Tears tumbled down her cheeks. 'What has he done?' she whimpered.

Chilcott and Foster caught each other's glances.

'We are still attempting to establish that fact, Mrs Coates,' Foster said softly. 'But it is fair to say that we are significantly concerned about your ex-husband and what he *may* have done.'

Chilcott watched in silence as the young woman before them finally broke down.

As Foster comforted Mrs Coates, Chilcott took the opportunity to break the news.

'I'm afraid your ex-husband has been arrested on suspicion of murder, Mrs Coates,' he said.

'Murder?' Mrs Coates said breathlessly. 'Murder?'

'I told you on the phone about the blood that was covering your ex-husband's body,' he said, snatching a peek at Foster. 'Well, it wasn't his blood. And in fact, we have established from forensic DNA analysis that it is likely to have come from at least one female, and probably two different female sources.'

Her eyes searched Chilcott's face with disbelieving confusion.

'I'm sorry to have to ask this question, but was your husband, sorry, ex-husband into kinky stuff? Swinging, threesomes, stuff like that?'

'Absolutely not.'

'One hundred per cent certain about that?'

Mrs Coates recoiled with a horrified expression that told Chilcott all he needed to know about his suggestion.

'Okay,' Foster intervened calmly. 'We aren't suggesting for a moment that we think this has happened.' She shot Chilcott a teacher-like glare. 'But we do need to establish who this blood belongs to.'

'He doesn't know anyone down here. At least, not that I'm aware of.'

'Okay,' Foster soothed. 'Do you mind if I ask the reason for your separation?'

'Is that necessary?'

'It will help us to understand your ex-husband, Mrs Coates. We have nothing to go on at the moment, and so long as he continues to be uncooperative, we aren't likely to understand. If we don't understand him, we can't help him.'

'It wasn't infidelity if that's what you're hoping for.'

'We aren't saying anything of the sort,' Foster reassured, as Chilcott's raised brow told a different story.

'I'm not gay,' Chilcott announced. 'But even I can see Travis is a good-looking man, and on top of that, he's a famous actor.'

Both Foster and Mrs Coates stared at him with deadpan expressions.

'Thank you for that, Robbie.'

'I'm just saying…'

'My husband is hardly famous. He was hoping this show would be his big opportunity to shine after all these years of struggling in the shadows of the more established actors. He's had plenty of supporting roles but nothing quite like this.'

'So then why did you separate?' Chilcott asked her directly.

Mrs Coates curled her lip as she stared at Chilcott.

'You probably think it's all glitz and glamour being an actor or being married to an actor. You couldn't be further from the truth. I rarely saw him. My two girls only knew their dad by his stage name. He was always away. Never at home. He earns a pittance for the work he puts in, which meant that I had to juggle two young daughters and whatever part-time jobs I could find, just to put clothes on their backs and food in their tummies.'

'Sounds familiar,' Chilcott muttered to himself.

'How old are your girls now?' Foster asked, shutting Chilcott out.

'Oh, um… seven and five.'

'Ah, lovely ages.'

'It's hard for them. It wasn't an easy decision to put my needs and the needs of my girls before Travis. But we did.'

She buried her face into her hands and began to weep loudly.

Happy now? Foster mouthed across to Chilcott, who raised his hands in innocence.

'Mrs Coates,' Foster soothed. 'Forgive my insensitive colleague.'

She aimed Chilcott another glower.

'We are as perplexed as you are about your ex-husband's situation.'

Mrs Coates looked up from her hands through bloodshot eyes. 'You must be wrong; Travis is a good man. He wouldn't hurt anyone.'

'Has he ever displayed any form of violence towards you?' Foster asked.

'No. Never. Travis is a loving, caring, thoughtful person. Our differences weren't because of the way he mistreated me. I loved him so much I couldn't bear to be away from him. And that was starting to destroy me. Do you know what that feels like? Do you?'

'I don't,' Foster said softly.

Chilcott cocked his head. 'I have to say, that doesn't

sound much like the person who we have been interviewing. He's arrogant, argumentative, self-centred—'

'Sounds like someone else I know,' Foster muttered just loud enough for Chilcott to hear.

'Are you sure you've got the right person?' Mrs Coates said.

'No, is the simple answer to that,' Foster said. 'We don't know who we've got in there. Because everything we've heard about Travis Yardley from you isn't the same as the person sitting in one of our cells.'

'He has to acknowledge who he really is,' Chilcott said. 'And take ownership for whatever he's done.'

Her eyes darted between Chilcott and Foster.

'Do you really think he's murdered someone?'

'We don't know,' Foster said. 'But we have to assume, going by the quantity of blood that we are presented with, that Travis has either taken part in or witnessed something resulting in significant injuries to another person or persons.'

'That's where you come in,' Chilcott said. 'We can't allow you to see him in person, but we'd quite like for you to watch his next interview from the satellite room and tell us what you think.'

'I can't see him? But I came all this way…'

'At the moment, you can't see him,' Foster said. 'But that could all change.'

'Why am I here if I can't see him?'

'I'm going to ask him some personal questions that only you and he would know the answer to,' Chilcott said. 'I want him to realise that we are in control, and we know more about him than he would have us believe.'

'I can't talk to him?' Mrs Coates repeated.

'No. Not at this time.'

'Before we get to the personal information, I wonder if you can help us out with any medical conditions he may have or any prescribed medications your ex-husband might be taking.'

'Um… nothing. My husband doesn't like taking pills. He's more into holistic therapies.'

Chilcott squinted. 'Such as?'

'Acupuncture… yoga, that sort of thing.'

'Do you have access to your ex-husband's emails?' DCI Foster asked.

'Not any longer. His agent deals with the business side of things.'

Chilcott poised his pen. 'Who is his agent, please?'

'Oh, uh… uh, it's Kate Lomax at Lomax and Grant Artists.'

'Based in…?'

'London.'

'How long has Miss Lomax been his agent?'

'For at least four years, I would guess.'

'Would she have set him up for this latest gig?'

'I assume so. Everything else goes through her.'

'How long were you and Travis married before you separated?' Chilcott continued.

'We were married for eleven years.'

'What are your children's names again?'

'Amelia and Lily-Belle.'

'Lovely names,' DCI Foster smiled.

'How did you meet?' Chilcott asked.

'We met at drama school.'

'And where did you honeymoon?' Chilcott said, still taking notes in his daybook.

'Travis was working in the States for a small production company at the time, so we combined his work with a short tour of the East Coast.'

'Is that where he got so good at the accent?' Foster said.

'Not really. He was always good with accents.'

'Any pets?' Chilcott asked.

Mrs Coates frowned. 'I don't understand. Why do you need to know these things about us?'

Chilcott lowered his pen and faced Mrs Coates.

'I need your husband to acknowledge who he is and what he has done. Knowing this information will prove to him we've done our homework, and he has nothing to hide – apart from the truth.'

'I don't understand why he just won't tell you?'

'Neither do we, Mrs Coates. That's why you are coming with us to Keynsham Custody Centre in a moment. It's time for you to meet Jesse Garcia.'

CHAPTER TWENTY

1:10 p.m.

The drive across the city was stop-start and painfully slow going, as was the conversation. Mrs Coates was only speaking when spoken to, and both Chilcott and Foster had exhausted their repertoire of small-talk. Of course, they had plenty to discuss, but the rear of a Ford Mondeo wasn't the most appropriate place for that to occur. Chilcott wasn't concerned, though. He knew as soon as Mrs Coates saw her ex-husband, everything would change.

'We will start by showing you clips from the interviews we have conducted so far,' Foster said. 'We can't show you everything as this is very much a live investigation and some things simply cannot be shared with members of the public.'

She looked back into the rear seats at a mute Mrs Coates, looking anything but comfortable with the situation.

'And then we'll see if it would be appropriate for you to see your ex-husband.'

'But I thought…?'

'Mrs Coates,' Chilcott said. 'We will be entering a secure custody unit. There are rules that even we have to adhere to. The custody sergeant will make the final decision whether you see your ex-husband or not. Or even if they'll allow you into the custody suite in the first instance. If something goes wrong, it's on their head, not ours.'

Chilcott glanced in the rear-view mirror. Mrs Coates was looking back at him with pleading eyes.

'We are putting our necks out, Mrs Coates,' Foster said. 'This is highly unusual. In fact, I've never done anything like this before.'

She looked at Chilcott, who shook his head.

'The first thing we must do is show you the interview footage and have you confirm that we are talking about the same person. Your ex-husband.'

'But you said—'

'Formality, Mrs Coates,' Foster said. 'Imagine we get you all this way only to find we aren't even talking about the same person.'

Mrs Coates dropped her head and remained in that position for the entirety of the rest of the journey.

Chilcott had left Foster inside the car with Mrs Coates as he went inside the custody unit to square away a private room for them to use. Luckily for him, the custody sergeant was someone he knew and gave the necessary permissions; on the proviso, Mrs Coates didn't leave Chilcott's sight while inside the custody unit.

He bounded back towards the car and came around to Foster's window, and she buzzed it down.

'All set,' he said. 'But we need to keep an eye on the time.'

'Right, come on, Mrs Coates, let's get this over with.'

They walked together through the various logging-in procedures and were escorted to a small room with video equipment.

'Please take a seat,' Chilcott said to Mrs Coates.

There was only one seat, front and centre of a sizeable wall-fixed TV monitor. Chilcott and Foster stood on either side, looking at the screen.

Chilcott lifted a hand controller, and the screen burst into life. He turned sideways and watched Mrs Coates. Her reaction told him everything. She was looking at her ex-husband.

'I'm going to press play, Mrs Coates. Please don't say anything until the footage has finished.'

She jiggled her head, somewhere between agreement and trepidation.

Chilcott hit the play button, and the voice of *Jesse Garcia* filled the room.

Chilcott had chosen a forty-two second-monologue. There was nothing of evidential value being said, but it was hopefully enough content to provoke a reaction from Mrs Coates. At the end, Chilcott paused the screen.

Mrs Coates had tears in her eyes and a look of total disbelief on her face.

'Tell us what you just saw.'

'I... I...' Mrs Coates struggled to speak. 'Why is Trav speaking like that?'

'What are you thinking,' Foster asked her.

'I… I don't know why he's being like that?'

'Is that your ex-husband?' Foster asked.

'Yes,' she whispered. '…um, but no. Not like that.'

'Any ideas why he's doing this?' Chilcott said.

Mrs Coates shook her head. She still hadn't taken her eyes from the screen.

'This is all we get from him,' Chilcott said. 'The same act throughout, no matter what we do. No matter what we ask.' He felt his phone vibrating in his pocket, and he took it out. It was the office. He killed the call and stuffed the phone back inside his trousers.

'Can you think of a way we can draw him out of this performance?'

Mrs Coates shook her head. 'I don't know?'

Chilcott's phone vibrated again.

'I'm sorry, just give me a moment. The office is keen to speak to me about something.'

He left the room, walked several paces along the corridor, and took the call.

'Hi, boss, it's Sean McEwan.'

'I'm a bit busy, son. Can this wait?'

'I thought you'd like to hear sooner rather than later, sir.'

'Okay, get on with it – what's so important?'

'I've just taken a call from a gentleman who says that he hypnotised Travis Yardley before the show in Bath.'

'Hypnotised?' That's just a load of rubbish, son.'

'It's not, boss. I've seen it in real life. It's amazing. The guy took someone from the audience and made him believe he was the queen. It was hilarious.'

'Stuff like that is set up for entertainment, Sean. I can't believe you fell for it.'

'Honestly, it's real.'

'Well, let's agree to disagree on that one. What does this so-called hypnotist say anyway?'

'He says that he made Yardley believe he was the character on stage. That he was Jesse Garcia in real life.'

Chilcott stopped walking.

'You what?'

'He says he hypnotised Travis Yardley into believing he was Jesse Garcia and made Yardley believe that he was a murderer.'

'Yes, I heard you first time, son. It was a rhetorical question.'

'Sorry, boss.'

Chilcott's face creased. 'Is that even possible?' he questioned himself aloud.

'I don't know, sir?'

'Who is this joker, this hypnotist?'

'I've taken all his details, and he checks out. He has a professional website and everything.'

There was a long silence as Chilcott considered the latest information.

'Sir?' DC McEwan prompted.

'I'm just thinking, son. It would make sense, but...'

'I've arranged to call him again. I wanted to update you first,' DC McEwan said.

Chilcott snapped from his daze. 'Good. What time are you calling him back?'

'I didn't give him a specific time, sir.'

'Wait for me to come back to the office. I want to speak to this hypnotist, see what he's got to say for himself.'

'How long will that be, sir?'

'I'll be there within the hour.'

CHAPTER TWENTY-ONE

Chilcott was with DC McEwan in his office, his desk phone on the loudspeaker.

'You called my colleague, Detective McEwan,' Chilcott said. 'You said something about hypnotising Travis Yardley. That's what I want to talk to you about.'

'Yes, I was in two minds if I should call or not.'

'Why was that?'

The hypnotist waited a few seconds before answering. 'I… I didn't want to get into any trouble.'

Chilcott chewed his inner cheek. 'Why did you call us?' he asked.

'I saw the news. I saw a detective inspector speaking to the cameras.'

'Yes, that was me.'

'Oh.'

'Yes, go on,' Chilcott said, rolling his eyes towards DC McEwan.

'It um… it wasn't until someone mentioned *his* name, and then I…' the man stopped talking.

'Travis Yardley.'

'Uh, yes,' the man replied.

'Try not to be nervous. Your information could be vital to us.'

The man didn't reply.

'Go on. You were saying?'

The hypnotist cleared his throat nervously, and Chilcott waved his hand at the phone. 'Look,' he said. 'Time is kind of important. If you have something to say, please just come out with it. We haven't got time for foreplay.'

'I… I um. I'm a… I'm a little concerned.'

'About?'

'I don't want to get into any trouble for what I've done.'

'Exactly, what have you done?'

The hypnotist didn't answer immediately, and Chilcott chomped down with a tightening jaw.

'What. Have. You. Done?'

'I, uh, I placed Mr Yardley into a state of deep hypnosis.'

Chilcott turned sideways to McEwan and raised a cynical brow.

'I… uh…' he stuttered. 'I basically turned Mr Yardley into his stage character.'

'Why?'

'Because he asked me to.'

Chilcott put his head into his hands.

'Um,' the hypnotist continued. 'Mr Yardley was very anxious about the current stage role.'

'How did you find him?'

'I didn't. He found me. I worked with him several years

ago, but then I didn't see him for a while. And then I received a call, we met up, and I assessed him.'

'Assessed him for what?'

'His hypnotic susceptibility.'

'Explain, please?'

'Hypnotic susceptibility is how willing and how easily a subject would be to hypnotise. I use a twelve-point scale to determine a subject's abilities.'

'Can't everyone be hypnotised?'

'No, not everyone. A subject has to be willing in the first place, and then their responses are measured on the scales of hypnotic susceptibility.'

'Okay – and how was Yardley on this scale?'

'He was capable of deep state hypnosis.'

'Meaning?'

'I had previously hypnotised him, he trusted in the process, so there was no resistance to the treatment. His desire to be hypnotised associated with his personal suscepti-bility made him an ideal subject.'

'I'm sorry, I'm a bit at a loss. I don't understand why Yardley wanted to be hypnotised in the first place?'

'For his art. He wanted to be the best he could be on stage. He, uh, well, he…' the hypnotist fumbled with his words. 'He wanted to make a good impression for the critics.'

'A good impression?'

'Yes.'

'So, you decided to turn him into a psychopathic killer?'

'Uh…' the hypnotist faltered. 'Yes. And no.'

'I'm not sure I believe any of this bullshit anyway,' Chilcott said dismissively, turning to DC McEwan.

'I'm sorry?' the hypnotist questioned.

'Hypnotism. Isn't it all set up with stooges in the audience?'

'I'm not sure where you get that impression, but I must inform you that hypnotism is most certainly real.'

'Yeah, right.'

'Hypnotism is absolutely authentic. It is used all over the world for the great benefit of many individuals, who otherwise, would fail in their personal quests—'

'To what?' Chilcott sneered. 'Become a murderer?'

'No, it wasn't like that at all. We had safety measures—'

'Safety measures – you mean like a word that would snap him out of his trance? Well, that clearly worked wonders, didn't it?'

The hypnotist didn't respond.

'What? If you've got something to say, you'd better say it now.'

'I didn't get to speak to him to confirm he was fully out of the hypnotic state. I left a message on his phone, and I have tried calling a number of times since, but he hasn't got back to me.'

'I was taking the piss about the keyword. Are you being serious?'

'Because we had previously worked together, I had built a strong connection with Mr Yardley. Having conditioned him face-to-face, so to speak, I was able to put him into a hypnotic state remotely.'

'You didn't see him personally?'

'No. I knew what time Mr Yardley was due to perform. I spoke to him on the phone, and then I would release him from his hypnosis after each show.'

'How could you do that if he was hypnotised?' Chilcott said, finding ways to discredit what the hypnotist was saying.

'It was part of the hypnosis. We had Mr Yardley's phone set to a specific ring tone for when I called. It was part of his conditioning that he would answer upon my call.'

'But you said that didn't happen on Saturday night?

'No. I couldn't get an answer, so I left the message on his voicemail.'

'So, what, you think he is still hypnotised to believe he is Jesse Garcia?'

'I'm afraid so.'

Chilcott scratched the top of his head and gave McEwan a sideways glance.

'How long had you been doing this for?'

'Uh, about three weeks. The theatre group travel all around the country. It wasn't practical for me to follow Mr Yardley around. I have a business to run.'

'Where are you based?'

'My practice is in Richmond.'

'Just talk me through the process again – you would call him, or he would call you?'

'He would call me from the theatre in the final hour before each performance.'

'And you would talk to him on the phone and place him into a trance.'

'Into hypnosis, yes.'

'Without seeing him?'

'Yes.'

'Don't you need some sort of visual stimulus?'

'No. Mr Yardley would respond to my voice and my

carefully-chosen words, and so a phone call was all we needed.'

'And so, during each show, he would be hypnotised?'

'Yes.'

'Until you brought back out of his hypnosis?'

'Yes.'

'And how would you do that?'

'Again, a sequence of words.'

'So, what went wrong this time?'

'I'm not saying it did go wrong. I left him a message when I couldn't get through to speak to him directly.'

'But you don't know for sure whether he did hear that message?'

'No.'

'Because you haven't heard from him since.'

'That's right.'

The hypnotist's voice was less confident.

'Well, I can tell you that the man in our custody centre believes he is Jesse Garcia, so I think we've got our answer – he didn't receive that message.'

'Oh, dear God!'

Chilcott looked at DC McEwan. 'I suppose we should thank our lucky stars he wasn't playing the lead role in *Shrek the Musical*.'

DC McEwan laughed behind his hands.

'Has he hurt someone?' the hypnotist asked timidly.

Chilcott squinted. 'Why would you ask that?'

'I… um…'

'Possibly. Probably.'

'Oh, God! Oh, dear God…' the hypnotist spluttered

Chilcott waited for a second or two.

'Something has just struck me. How can he remember his lines if he is hypnotised on stage?'

'Because I conditioned him to remember everything he was meant to say, when to say it, and how to react according to the script. Only, he would do it with the total belief that he *was* Jesse Garcia.'

'But, if that was for the stage with you basically telling him what to do, why would he continue to believe he was Jesse Garcia afterwards?'

'In the moments upon the stage, his hypnotised self was balanced. There was absolutely no risk that he would do anything he shouldn't.'

'And away from the stage?'

Several seconds went by before the hypnotist spoke.

'Away from the stage, he would still be Jesse Garcia, but he wouldn't be following a script.'

'So, he would be under the belief he was a murderer until you bring him out of his hypnotic state?'

'Kind of. A hypnotist cannot make someone do something against their free will.'

'Meaning what?'

'The actions an individual takes while in a state of hypnosis are still balanced by their individual beliefs and considerations of what is right or wrong.'

Chilcott pulled a face. 'Okay, so we get you down here with us, and you do whatever it is that you need to do to get Yardley out of his hypnosis so that we can get some sense out of him and find out exactly what the bloody hell he has done?'

'Um…' the hypnotist hesitated.

Chilcott creased his brow. 'Yes?'

'It's not that straightforward.'

'What isn't? You'll come to the custody centre. We make sure you are safe and all that, and then you say what you need to say to bring Travis Yardley back into the room, or however you term it?'

DC McEwan scoffed behind his hand once again.

'Um, you want to question him about what he has done during his hypnotic state?'

'Uh… hello? He was covered in someone else's blood. I think that would be a damn good place to start, don't you?'

'He won't remember. He is conditioned to forget everything once he regains full independent consciousness.'

'You what? Just run that last little bit by me again.'

'He won't remember a thing about what has happened since being placed into his hypnotic state. He will have total amnesia about everything. It's one of the safety measures to ensure he doesn't drift somehow back into character.'

'Are you telling me that if we bring that man out of his hypnotic state, he won't remember a single bloody thing about what he has done, who he has done it to, or where he has done it?'

'Exactly that.'

Chilcott leant his elbows on the desk and buried his face into his hands.

CHAPTER TWENTY-TWO

DCI Foster stared incredulously at her DI, but Chilcott did nothing but keep his face firmly implanted in the palms of his hands. He knew that if he let them loose, he was sure to lash out at the nearest object or person, and he didn't want to deal with the fallout from either of those two scenarios.

'What you're telling me is that even if we brought Travis Yardley out of his hypnotic state, he isn't going to remember a single thing about where he has been or what he has done?'

Chilcott slid both hands slowly down his face and grunted his reply.

'Christ, Robbie. Why do you always have to find the hard route to follow.'

'I wish I'd never answered the bloody phone,' he muttered.

The DCI stood and stared for a long minute out through the window.

'We've got difficult decisions to make,' she said.

'We?'

'Yes,' she said turning to Chilcott. 'We.'

'About what in particular?'

'Quite,' she said, returning to her seat. 'We have a few difficult decisions to make.'

Chilcott sat back and cupped his hands behind his head. It was one of those body gestures that could be interpreted in a number of ways. In some cases, it could be construed as being self-assured, cocky even. But on this occasion, it symbolised defeat.

'What do we do with Yardley, or should I be saying Garcia?' she said. 'Do we let the hypnotist into the custody centre and ask him to break the spell?'

'If we do that, we lose all hope of finding our victims,' Chilcott said down to the floor. 'I've been through this a hundred times already.'

'And what did you conclude?'

Chilcott looked up at his boss. 'I haven't yet.'

The DCI turned her back, looked out through the window.

'When Yardley wakes up, he won't have a clue what's going on or why he's in police custody. I almost feel sorry for the bloke.'

'What about the hypnotist?'

'What about him?'

'Is he culpable? Should we consider him as an accomplice? Even a naïve conspirator?'

Chilcott shrugged. 'Probably not, in the eyes of the law. He was providing a service upon request, and no matter how fucked up we may think that is, he couldn't have foreseen whatever has happened.'

'That's the part that really bothers me. We still don't know what has happened – if anything?'

'Trust me. It's happened alright.'

'So, we know about this character, the one from the show. We know his fictional MO. I can't understand why can't we locate his victims?'

'Because we're looking in the wrong places.'

'I'm all ears, Robbie. Tell me the right places.'

'If I knew that, we wouldn't be here debating the facts right now.'

'Okay,' she said, coming back to her desk. 'Let's not overcomplicate this anymore than it already is. First, we'll stick it to Yardley, or Garcia, depending on who we think we have in our cells. It's time to play our trump card.'

'Christ! You're optimistic! What card might that be, then?'

'We'll toss Mrs Coates into the mix. Let him see her. Let him speak to her.'

'Hoping for?'

'If he is completely hypnotised, as suggested, then presumably we shouldn't see any form of reaction from Travis Yardley. But if he shows so much as a twitch of recognition at the sight of seeing her, then we need to re-think our tactics and dismiss what the hypnotist has told us.'

'Okay, but let me run that by the hypnotist first, just so that we know what to expect. The last thing we want to do is create another bloody incident and a third victim.'

'Fine. But I want you with me in the satellite room. I want to test Yardley to make sure that the reason he isn't talking is because he's taken a dislike to you.'

Chilcott pulled a face. 'Why would he do that?'

Foster gave him a knowing look.

'It's your call.'

Chilcott made for the exit and stopped himself short.

'And the second?' he asked.

'The second?'

'You said, "*First we'll stick it to Yardley*", so what's the second plan?'

She gave Chilcott a lingering stare.

'You don't need to worry about that right now.'

CHAPTER TWENTY-THREE

Chilcott stood by the door in silence, watching the TV screen as DC McEwan and DC Fowler interviewed Travis Yardley once again. Mrs Coates was sitting in front of the large monitor, and it took until about five minutes in before she tore her eyes from the screen and turned to Chilcott.

'Why is he being like this?'

'So, you think he is acting differently?' Chilcott said.

'Totally. He looks like Travis, but that's as far as it goes. Everything else about him is different.'

'I understand.'

'Why does she keep calling him Jesse?' Mrs Coates asked.

'As you can probably tell, Travis has assumed the identity of someone he knows well: the character he was playing in his show. Calling him by that name is a tactic we use during interviews to indulge a suspect.'

'Is he schizophrenic?'

Chilcott blinked. He already knew the answer. He was just testing Mrs Coates' reaction.

'Possibly,' he said, 'or… maybe not.'

She looked at him sadly.

'There's a suggestion that at this time, Travis is hypnotised, and he believes he is, in fact, Jesse Garcia.'

'What?' Mrs Coates said.

'Has he done anything like that before, being hypnotised?'

'Uh… yes. A while ago now.'

'Tell me about that.'

'Travis has always been fame-hungry but never broken through to the big time. He tried various coaches to improve his acting, but nothing worked out the way he wanted. And then I heard about this guy who had helped actors by using hypnotism.'

'So, Travis used him?'

'Yes. We both did.'

'And did it work?'

'For a time, yes.'

'But he still didn't get a breakthrough role?'

Mrs Coates shook her head and looked back at the screen.

'We think he has used the hypnotist again, Mrs Coates. But he hasn't come out of the trance.'

She put a hand to her mouth, watching the screen as DC Fowler delivered several more tactical questions.

'Why was he in his underwear?' Mrs Coates asked after a further minute viewing her ex-husband.

Chilcott offered her a sympathetic smile.

'We don't know, and we haven't recovered the remainder of his clothing yet.'

Chilcott could see moisture in her eyes reflected from the

monitor's light. The video had to be hard to watch, but it wasn't about to get any easier for the poor woman.

'Mrs Coates, did your ex-husband have any female friends in the Bath area?'

She turned quickly to face him. 'Friends? You mean sexual partners, don't you?'

'Yes. I do.'

'No, of course not. As far as I was aware, we didn't have any friends in this area. Male or female.'

Chilcott cleared his throat with a single cough.

'Mrs Coates,' he said. 'I'm going to break all the rules here, and I want you to see your ex-husband in person.'

'Oh, God. That would be so good. Thank you.'

'It's not a social visit. I want to see how he responds to you.'

'You'll be watching?'

'We can't leave you unattended for any number of reasons, not least your safety. But I want you to go into the interview room with my colleagues, and I want your ex-husband to see you.'

Mrs Coates dabbed at her eyes with a tissue.

'It will only be for a brief moment, I'm afraid. It would be best if you didn't say anything to him. We just want Travis to see you.'

Mrs Coates looked confused. 'Why?'

'It will really help us, Mrs Coates. But most of all, it could really help Travis too.'

Mrs Coates hesitated; then nodded.

'Stay here for a moment,' Chilcott said, touching her arm. 'And I'll be back soon.'

He left the satellite room and made directly for the interview, where he paused the proceedings and explained to DC McEwan what was about to happen.

He bounded back to the satellite room. 'Okay, Mrs Coates, if you'd like to follow me, please.'

They walked the short corridor, and Chilcott met DC McEwan just outside the door and handed over Mrs Coates to him.

'Give me two minutes to get back to the screen and then take Mrs Coates inside the room and make sure Yardley sees her.'

'Yes, boss. Then what?'

'Nothing. Let him see her. Assess his reaction and take it from there.'

Chilcott hurried back and settled into his seat. Right on cue, the interview room door opened and in walked DC McEwan with Mrs Coates close behind. DC McEwan introduced Mrs Coates for the benefit of the recording equipment, and they stood alongside one another, just in front of the door.

Chilcott leaned in closer towards the TV screen, staring intently at Yardley, begging him for a reaction.

Yardley peered impassively at the new occupant with not so much as a glimmer of recognition, let alone emotion.

'Mr Garcia,' DC McEwan said, playing along with his identity crisis. 'Do you recognise this woman?'

He blinked and lifted one of his eyebrows. 'Nope. Should I?'

Chilcott watched Mrs Coates shiver at the coldness of the comment.

'Trav, it's me,' she whimpered.

'Who the fuck is Trav?' Yardley asked, leaning in

towards his solicitor while practically ignoring the presence of his ex-wife in the room.

Mrs Coates flinched, and DC McEwan whispered encouragement in her ear.

'My client would like to know the reason why this person has been introduced to him?' the solicitor said

'This is Georgia Coates. She is the ex-wife of Travis Yardley.'

DC McEwan left it hanging in the air like a bad smell.

'Pah,' Yardley spluttered.

'Trav? Why are you doing this?' Mrs Coates questioned, stepping forwards.

'Are you saying you have never met this woman before?' DC McEwan asked Yardley.

Yardley pulled a pained expression. 'She's not my type. You know what I'm saying, bro?'

'Can't you do something?' Mrs Coates pleaded, turning to DC McEwan with desperation in her eyes. 'Can't you make him Travis again?'

DC McEwan attempted to calm Mrs Coates down, but she was becoming louder and increasingly agitated.

'Make him Travis again. Get him back. Make Travis great again. Just make Travis great again.' She began crying loudly and buried herself into the arms of DC McEwan.

'Thank you, I think it is time Mrs Coates left the interview room,' DC McEwan said.

Chilcott ran down the corridor and intercepted Mrs Coates on her way out.

'Well done,' he said. 'I know that was hard, but we needed to confirm our suspicions.'

Mrs Coates' broken face peered up at him. 'Of what?'

'That your ex-husband was in a state of hypnotism.'

'Do you think he is?'

'We do. Please don't feel bad about what just happened. We had to know, and this was one way of finding out.'

'You used me.'

'No. We didn't. We don't know Travis. You do. You know how he acts; you know how he is when he sees you. And that wasn't him, was it?'

She shook her head.

'Does it surprise you that he used a hypnotist again?'

She made a slight grunting noise and then answered, 'Not really. His acting is everything to him. More than his own sodding family.'

As they walked slowly back towards the satellite room, Mrs Coates said, 'He didn't know me. It was like I didn't exist.'

'Please don't take it personally. He's clearly not himself.'

She stopped walking and turned to Chilcott. 'What are you going to do with him?'

'We have to continue asking him questions as we find more evidence.'

'Of what?'

Chilcott looked away.

'Just exactly what do you think Travis has done?'

Chilcott scratched his bottom lip, giving himself a second or two to think about his answer. 'I'm going to be honest, Mrs Coates. It's not looking good for Travis. There was a lot of blood. A lot of blood,' he said to re-emphasise the point. 'We still don't know who it came from or where they are now.'

Mrs Coates stared at him wide-eyed.

'His cooperation is crucial, but you've seen for yourself what we get from him. We can't help him until he starts helping himself.'

'It's like… it's like it's not him,' Mrs Coates said. 'He's somebody else.'

'He is.'

'So how can Travis be in trouble if it's not him?'

Chilcott scratched behind his ear. 'There we go. There's our dilemma. I am sure Travis is a decent man—'

'He is. He is.'

'But the man sitting in there is almost certainly not a good man.'

'But it is Trav,' she implored. 'It's still him.'

'Maybe on the outside.'

'Can't you just bring him out of the hypnotism?'

'We could. But then we'd lose any chance of that man sitting in that room right now, telling us what he's done and where to find the victims. And that's not a luxury we can currently afford.'

'That's madness.'

'The same way he can't remember you at the moment is the same way he won't remember any of this once he's brought out of his hypnotic state.'

'It's unfair to keep him like this. You can't.'

Chilcott looked down, studied his shoes.

'To some, maybe it is unfair, but we're out of luck with any other options, and we need to find those victims. Garcia has the answers we are looking for, and unfortunately, your ex-husband does not.'

Mrs Coates curled up into a tight ball.

'We are going to bring him around as soon as we

possibly can. We've been in touch with the hypnotist who treated Travis, and it is all set up for him to bring him out of the trance.'

'You've what?'

'We're just waiting for the right moment.'

'To bring Travis back?'

'Yes, to bring Travis back.'

'When will that be?'

'Soon.'

'I want to go home,' Mrs Coates sobbed. 'Please. I just want to go home.'

'I'll have someone take you back to the hotel. But I'd like you to stick around the area until the hypnotist has done his thing if that's okay? You are the only person who can tell if Travis is back to his old self. Nobody else here knows him as you do.'

'I'm going home tomorrow, and you can't stop me. That isn't Trav in there, and you have no right to keep him that way.'

CHAPTER TWENTY-FOUR

4:44 p.m.

Twenty-three hours, twenty-one minutes until custody time limits expire.

Chilcott and DCI Foster stood beside the incident board. They had reached the point where a tough decision was needed. Yardley had so far spent seventy-two hours twenty-four minutes cooped up in the cell. The problem was, both Chilcott and Foster knew this investigation still had a marathon to run before Yardley could cross the line.

Chilcott leaned in close to Foster. 'Should we release him now – keep some time in the bank for when we eventually find a victim?'

Foster continued staring up at the timeline.

This case was unlike any other. Typically, the police would have a starting point: a victim, a crime scene, the modus operandi, and a wealth of evidence to work from in reverse fashion, not so with this case. The starting point was somewhere at the end, with Travis Yardley fleeing the scene of the crime. Wherever that might be?

She shook her head and rubbed her weary face with a hand.

'I don't know. I just don't know.'

'We won't get a charging decision from CPS. No way. As it stands, there's not enough evidence to charge him with murder, and there aren't any offences that I know of for being found with someone else's blood on your body.'

Foster let out a defeated sigh. 'It could be worse than that.'

Chilcott faced her.

'He might have a defence in law.'

'He might have a what?'

'Automatism.'

'Come again.'

'In law, a defendant must pursue a voluntary act to establish the *actus reus* of a crime. He must also be conscious of his act providing the *mens rea*. Our man has neither the guilty act nor the guilty mind because it wasn't him at the time. He was hypnotised.'

'No. I'm not buying into that. If someone is pissed out of their head or high on drugs, it doesn't give them a defence for their criminal actions. It's the same here. He asked to get hypnotised. He wanted to become a killer, even if it was for a stage show. He's guilty of whatever criminal act we find him to have done.'

'Which so far is nothing.'

Chilcott stroked his forehead with a clawed hand. 'It's your call, Julie. You're the boss.'

'We aren't going to get *Garcia* to cough anything up. Contact the hypnotist. I think it's time we met Travis Yardley.'

'Are you sure? That's a big call.'

'I'm sure all we are doing is wasting time – time that we certainly don't have on our side.'

A mobile phone was placed in the centre of the table, the volume up high, the setting on loudspeaker. The hypnotist was ready to do his thing at the other end of the line. Travis Yardley was seated in the interview room, his hands cuffed together, his solicitor alongside him maintaining a silent counsel. The hypnotist had insisted that Yardley not have a police presence during the procedure. Still, Chilcott was taking no chances, and two detention officers were waiting outside of the closed door, ready to burst in, if and when needed. Chilcott and Foster sat in front of the TV monitor, neither of them knowing quite what to expect. This was unchartered territory.

The hypnotist began his patter. He spoke so softly that Chilcott could hardly hear him through the video. His voice was different from the timid and anxious one that Chilcott had heard earlier that evening. Now, the hypnotist was calm. He was authoritative. He was controlling.

'This is something we don't see every day,' Chilcott muttered to Foster.

'Sshh,' she said. 'Listen to what he's saying.'

They could see directly towards Yardley's face. His eyes

were closed, as were his instructions, and he was motionless in the chair.

'I'm going to count slowly backwards from ten to one,' the hypnotist said. 'As I get closer to one, you will gradually feel more alert. You will gradually begin to wake up.' He paused for a moment. 'Ten… nine… eight…'

'Oh, just get on with it,' Chilcott shouted to the TV screen.

'You are starting to feel awake now…four …three, open your eyes…'

Foster and Chilcott leaned in closer to the large screen and saw Yardley open his eyes as requested.

'Don't be alarmed. You are in a safe environment,' the hypnotist said. And two… and one.'

Yardley blinked and jerked his head back. He tugged at the restraints on his wrists and looked around the room, his head lurching from left to right.

'It's okay,' the hypnotist said calmly. 'You're in a safe place. You are perfectly safe.'

'Get in there,' Foster told Chilcott, but he was already out of the door.

CHAPTER TWENTY-FIVE

'Thanks, I'll take it from here,' Chilcott said, lifting the phone from the centre of the table. 'An officer is going to call you back to take a quick statement about what you've just done.'

'Can't I—'

'No. You cannot. I think you've done quite enough.' He killed the call with a stiff finger and stared blankly at Yardley.

DC Fowler came into the interview room and joined Chilcott's side.

'What the hell is happening?' Yardley asked breathlessly.

'You are under arrest in Keynsham Custody Centre,' Chilcott replied.

'Arrested?'

Chilcott sat down opposite Yardley and drew in a deep breath. He looked long and hard at the man opposite him. Unbelievably, it was like looking at a completely different person.

Yardley pulled at his handcuffs, staring wide-eyed at Mr Wilson, who was taking notes alongside him.

'I suppose we can take those off you now.' He leaned forward and took hold of the bridge of Yardley's handcuffs. 'Keep still, and I'll have these off in a second.'

Chilcott fiddled with the key in the hole and released the first wrist from the shackles.

Yardley shook his hand to get the circulation of blood flowing again.

'Just place your hand flat on the table, please,' Chilcott instructed as he went about releasing Yardley's other wrist. 'I don't want any surprises.'

'What am I doing here?' Yardley pleaded – his eyes wide and fearful.

'Firstly, I need to inform you that this conversation is being video recorded. I am Detective Inspector Robbie Chilcott, and I am leading the investigation. My colleague here is Detective Fowler. The man seated beside you is your solicitor, Mr Wilson.'

'My solicitor?' Yardley said, looking at Mr Wilson with a concerned expression.

'What is your full name?'

'Uh… I'm known as Travis Yardley, but… but that's not my real name.'

'Which is?'

'Elliott,' he said, still looking around the room and at Chilcott, Fowler and Mr Wilson.

'Elliott John Coates?' Chilcott prompted.

'Yea…yes.'

'And you are an actor known predominantly by your stage name.'

'Yea… uh…'

'Fine. Are you happy for us to refer to you as Travis Yardley for the purposes of this conversation?'

Yardley nodded. 'Yes, please. It's only my mother who calls me Elliott these days.' He forced a nervous smile.

'Do you remember anything about the last few days?' Chilcott said, ignoring Yardley's attempt to lighten the mood.

'Days?' Yardley squeaked. 'No,' he said almost in tears.

Chilcott glanced at DC Fowler 'Right, just to confirm. You have no recollection of why you are here?'

'No. None. What's going on?'

Chilcott sniffed and pushed a hot polystyrene cup of sugary tea towards Yardley.

'I didn't know how you took it. Leave it if you don't fancy any.'

Yardley looked down but barely registered the cup in front of him.

'You've been arrested on suspicion of murder.'

Yardley froze apart from his jaw, which had dropped wide open.

'You were found on a country road. You were covered in someone else's blood – female's blood. And due to the significant quantity of blood found upon you, we suspect that serious harm has been caused to at least one female.'

'Wha… Uh…'

Chilcott watched Yardley's reaction with a keen eye.

'Wh… who… is she?' Yardley whimpered.

'We were hoping you could tell us that?'

Small gasps came from Yardley's mouth, but not enough to form words.

'You were hypnotised. Do you recall that?'

Yardley's eyes searched around the room like a caged animal in a veterinary practice. The impact of Chilcott's words had not yet sunk in.

'Mr Yardley. Do you remember being hypnotised?'

'Yes.'

'When was that?'

Yardley's eyes darted between Chilcott and DC Fowler.

'Earlier this evening?'

'You've been with us here in police custody for the last three days, son.'

Yardley's disbelieving stare fixed on Chilcott's face.

'Can't be…' he mouthed.

'Trust me, son. You have.'

Chilcott watched as Yardley began to process the information. He didn't speak. He didn't want to overwhelm the man any more than he already had.

'What happened?' Yardley questioned, sinking his head into his hands.

'You met a female after last Saturday's show at Bath's Theatre Royal. You took a taxi with the female somewhere near Hinton Charterhouse, where you were picked up a couple of hours later.'

Chilcott studied Yardley's vacant reactions. It was apparent he was hearing this information for the first time.

'You were semi-naked, wearing only boxer shorts. And we believe you were covered in her blood.'

'Wha…?'

Yardley's skin was turning a shade of ashen grey.

Chilcott and Fowler stayed quiet as they watched Yardley's internal suffering come to the surface.

'Oh my God,' he muttered.

He looked up at Chilcott. 'But it couldn't be…'

Chilcott acknowledged the comment. 'You were under a state of hypnotism. You believed you were Jesse Garcia.'

'That's my character… in the show that I'm in,' Yardley attempted to explain.

'We know. We also know that you were placed into a hypnotic state at around 6 p.m. on the night of the show last Saturday, and you were never brought back out of it. And here we all are as a result.'

'No, that's not right.'

'Trust me, son. We've just watched as your hypnotist has brought you back around. Two minutes ago, you were still Jesse Garcia.'

'I… I, I don't know what's happening… really, I have no idea.'

Chilcott scratched his head. 'If I hadn't just witnessed that with my own eyes, I don't think I would have believed it?'

Yardley tugged at his long straight dark hair. 'I don't understand, he murmured. 'I did come out of the hypnotism.'

'No. You didn't.' Chilcott sniffed loudly and sighed. 'Anyway, the bottom line is we need to find that girl. You need to help us find that girl.'

Yardley's lips moved, but no sound came out. Tears trickled down into the corners of his mouth.

'I don't know how.'

CHAPTER TWENTY-SIX

Chilcott sat alone at his desk. The door was closed, and the lights were off. He clutched the back of his head, his elbows weighing heavy on the tabletop. How could the investigation have become such a monumental cock up? And what was he to do about Yardley? The man clearly had no recollection, but he'd brought it upon himself, which made him more than culpable for his actions if Chilcott could find the bloody victim.

A double-tap on the door shattered Chilcott's lethargy, and he responded without looking behind. 'Yes, what is it?'

'Um, sorry to disturb you, sir,' Detective Phillips said, gingerly hesitating in the doorway, 'but, you have a visitor.'

'Not now, Fleur. Tell them to come back another time.'

DC Phillips didn't answer, and seconds later, Chilcott became aware of somebody standing beside his desk. He cranked his head sideways and looked up at the visitor through the mask of his hands.

'I know what happened,' the visitor said. 'I know where to find them.'

Chilcott slowly released his head from the warming comfort of his hands. He leaned back and looked with disdain at the man standing beside him. He stared at him for a good long minute.

'I don't need any help,' he said.

'From where I'm standing, I'd have to disagree.'

'Let me put it another way,' Chilcott said, tightening up. 'I don't need any help from the likes of you.'

The man returned a dead stare. 'I think you do. And I know you know it.'

Chilcott jumped up from his seat and glared defiantly at the visitor.

'When I want help. I'll ask for help. And trust me, you'll be the last person to hear about it.'

The man nodded and slowly looked around the room before resting his eyes on the incident board through the office's glass walls.

'You need me,' he said calmly. 'The victims need me.'

'I don't need you. But if I decided I did need you one day, I'd get on the phone and call you. Until that time, if you don't mind, I'm kind of busy trying to solve a complex case.'

'It's a murder,' the visitor corrected Chilcott, and then he shook his head. 'No. It's two murders.'

Chilcott squinted and glanced towards DC Phillips, who was still waiting beside the door.

'Thank you for taking an interest in my investigation. I'll be sure to bear you in mind, should the need arise. Until that time, if you please…' Chilcott held an outstretched arm towards the open door and a puzzled-looking DC Phillips.

The visitor didn't speak. He gave Chilcott a once-over

and slowly walked towards the door and beyond an open-mouthed DC Phillips.

Ten seconds passed, and then Phillips said, 'But, sir… that was—'

'I know exactly who that was, Fleur.'

Phillips looked over towards the exit and the man disappearing from view.

'Am I missing something here, sir?' she asked hesitantly.

Chilcott looked at her blankly and answered as if the preceding conversation hadn't taken place. 'Missing something like what, Fleur?'

'That was…'

'I know.'

'But… but…'

'But what? What exactly do you expect me to do?'

'But… what if he can help us, sir. What if he does know something?'

Chilcott sniffed the air and sat back down in his seat, not taking his eyes off Phillips.

'Don't tell me you've been sucked in by all the hype as well?'

Phillips twitched her head with uncertainty.

'Come on, Fleur. Seriously? Of all the detectives who I trust in this place. You of all people…'

Phillips blinked several times and stepped further into the office. She stood where the visitor had been standing and looked back into the incident room and the board on the wall showing the limited timeline of events. She stared for a long, challenging moment, turned, gave her boss one final disapproving look and then left the room without further comment.

He waited until she was gone from view and then stood up and closed the office door with defiant purpose. He returned to his seat and looked out into the incident room at the team of detectives going diligently about their business.

He twiddled his biro between his fingers for a moment and pondered the brief encounter before his eyes locked onto the incident board and the limited timeline of evidence.

Who have you been talking to, DC Deans?

'It appears your guest has created quite a stir,' DCI Foster commented as she offered her troubled DI a seat in her office.

'Freak shows tend to have that effect,' Chilcott answered.

Foster interlocked her fingers and leant on her elbows as she stared sideways for a long moment at him.

'What did he say?' she asked.

'Who?'

Foster raised a brow. 'DC Deans, of course. What could he offer?'

Chilcott spluttered as he answered. 'You're kidding, aren't you?'

Foster slowly unclamped her hands.

'Oh, no… what have you done?'

'What do you mean?'

'I get the feeling I'm not going like what comes out of your mouth next.'

'What? I haven't done anything. Why do you always think the worst of me?'

Chilcott turned away sheepishly.

'Because I know you.'

He didn't respond and brushed imaginary lint from his thighs.

'Robbie. What have you said to Andy Deans?'

'Nothing.'

Chilcott adjusted himself in the seat.

'I just told him we didn't need him.'

Foster dropped her forehead into her hands.

'What?'

'I asked him to come,' she said down at her desktop. 'He called me this afternoon and told me he had information that could help our investigation.'

She looked over at Chilcott. 'And I invited him over from Falcon Road CID to see what he had to say.'

'Well, nobody told me. Don't you think that I should have known about this too?'

'I didn't think I'd have to run it by you, Robbie. After all, the last time I checked, I was still in charge of this department.'

'I'm just saying, it might have helped for me to know he was coming.'

Chilcott noticed his boss's annoyed glare.

'That's all I'm saying.'

'Get him back.'

'No.'

Foster forced her eyes wide uncompromisingly. 'Get him back. I need to know what he has to say.'

'He's a joke,' Chilcott said, screwing up his face.

'He is not a joke. He is a valuable asset that we are lucky to have in our constabulary.'

Chilcott puffed out air mockingly.

'Where have your traditional methods got us, Robbie? Exactly how much closer are you to solving this case than when this all started?'

Chilcott rolled his eyes and folded his arms defensively.

'Anyway,' he said. 'I didn't think you used the phrase *traditional methods* in the same sentence as my name?'

Foster agreed.

'You're right. I can hardly describe you as a text-book detective, but that doesn't mean we can't at least explore other methods and sources of evidence.'

'I just can't understand why you had to feed him details about the case.'

'What do you mean?'

'The DNA traces – why tell him there were two blood types?'

Foster blinked. 'I didn't. I haven't disclosed any evidence to Detective Deans whatsoever.'

She paused for a few seconds. 'Why do you say that?'

'It's nothing,' Chilcott shrugged.

'Well, clearly, it is *something* for you to mention it in the first place. Tell me what he said.'

Chilcott rocked his head. 'He just mentioned it was murder. Two murders. I assumed you had told him about the two DNA hits, and he took a punt on a lucky guess.'

Foster covered her mouth with a balled fist and didn't take her eyes from Chilcott.

'Get him back,' she said. 'Get him back right now.'

CHAPTER TWENTY-SEVEN

DCI Foster didn't know DC Andy Deans personally, but she had followed his career closely since his tragic circumstances had been so widely scrutinised and shared around the globe. Since that time, Deans had become something of a cult figure within the force, and his name was spoken with hushed reverence in the corridors, tea rooms and squad cars.

Foster didn't know which side of the fence she sat on regarding his supposed *abilities*, but she was always willing to give everyone a break, and that was something this case needed desperately.

She greeted him alone, deciding it was pertinent not to include Chilcott at this stage.

'Thank you so much for coming back, Andy. I can only apologise for the misunderstanding earlier.'

'That's okay, Ma'am,' Deans said. 'The traffic wasn't so bad coming back.'

Foster smiled apologetically.

'How are you?' she asked.

'I'm good. Thank you.'

Foster scratched the lobe of her ear, holding on to her smile as long as possible.

'It's okay,' Deans said. 'There's no need to be different around me.'

'I'm just sorry we haven't made acquaintances before,' Foster said, thinking quickly of something to say.

'Me too. But it's a pleasure to meet you now, Ma'am.'

'Please, call me Julie.'

She looked back towards the door. 'Unless we're with the junior team – you know, appearances and all.'

They stood for an awkward moment, and then she offered him a chair.

'Do you know why I called you over?' she said as they took their seats.

'You need help with the Hinton Charterhouse case.'

'Yes, we do.'

Deans looked around the office and then at the DCI's clear desk.

'My DI has all the information we need,' she said.

Deans squinted. 'Okay. Does he know I've come back?'

'Yes, he does. And he also knows how I feel about you being sent away in the first place.'

Deans tilted his head.

'He told me that you know there are two victims.'

'There are.'

'How did you know that?'

Deans stared at Foster but didn't answer.

'It's okay; I'm open-minded,' she said.

Deans contemplated his answer for a second or two.

'I saw it,' he said.

'You saw it?' she repeated. 'How exactly did you see it?'

'In a dream.'

Deans looked down and away.

'It's hard for me to explain *how* I see…' He looked back at Foster. 'You just need to trust me.'

Foster hesitated. 'Exactly, what did you see?'

DC Deans inhaled a long steady breath and moistened his lips with his tongue. He gave Foster a final assessing look.

'The first victim was premeditated. He lured her to her death. The second murder was out of necessity.'

Foster leaned towards Deans. 'Who are they?' she asked firmly.

'Both females.'

Foster leaned back against the upright of her chair.

'How did you know that?'

Deans stood up and walked towards the glass wall of the office, and looked out into the incident room. 'They live together,' he said softly. 'I see a big house and an outbuilding.'

'Where?'

'I'll know when I see it.'

'*Who* are they?'

Deans stared ahead silently for a moment and then turned around.

'I think they could be related. Perhaps mother and daughter.'

'A child?'

'No. Both adults.'

Foster stood up and walked over to where Deans was standing.

'How did he do it – our suspect?'

'He stabbed them both with a knife.'

'What sort of knife?'

'A kitchen knife. Stainless steel. Broad handle. Ten-inch blade, maybe longer.'

She hovered for a beat and then peered out into the incident room; the same way Deans had looked.

'He...' Deans said, covering his mouth with a hand. 'It was a savage attack.'

Foster continued to stare out through the glass. 'Okay,' she said softly. 'How can we evidence what you've manifested? How can we make this tangible? How can we make this work for the investigation?'

'By finding the victims.'

'And you can do that?'

Deans turned to her. 'I've seen it all,' he said. 'I've seen the crime through the eyes of the victim.'

'You've seen the crime scene?'

'Yes.'

'Can you take us to the crime scene?'

'I'll know when I know.'

'Are the victims in Hinton Charterhouse? Can you tell me that much?'

'I believe so. That's a good starting point.'

'Right,' she said, walking briskly to her desk. 'That's near your patch, isn't it – near Bath?'

'Nearby, yes. But not my jurisdiction.'

'Don't worry about district boundaries. The major crime investigation team is constabulary wide, and you're working for us now.'

'I want you to take DI Chilcott and one of his team to Hinton Charterhouse tonight. I want you to drive around until you recognise, sense, tingle, or feel whatever it is you perceive. And I want you to find our victims.'

'Yes, Ma'am.'

'Don't come back until you do. Is that understood?'

'Yes, Ma'am.'

'Good. Now, let's go and break the news to DI Chilcott.'

'I'm doing what?' Chilcott said, spitting hot coffee over his hand as he slurped from a mug.

'Don't hang around here arguing the toss about it,' Foster said. 'We're wasting valuable time.'

'As opposed to wasting valuable time entraining some fruitcake on a drive around?'

Foster glared at him.

'Well, come on…' Chilcott said, expecting an answer.

'Just do it, will you?'

Chilcott grunted. 'Who else do you want me to take? Who else can we sacrifice for this bullshit enquiry?'

'That's up to you. So long as DC Deans calls the shots, I don't care who else you take. Just get on with it. We've got a crime scene to find.'

'Bullshit,' Chilcott shouted. 'This is utter bullshit.' He looked out through the gap in the office door and saw DC Deans standing on the other side.

'You're wasting time,' Foster said, tapping her watch face as if her statement needed reinforcing.

'Your Honour,' Chilcott boomed theatrically. 'It matters not that we have no evidence of a murder. Detective Deans has seen the crime play out in the mysterious ether of time, and he can identify the offender from the shadows of darkness…'

'Grow up, will you.'

Chilcott huffed and scooped up a set of car keys.

'I'm driving,' he said, stomping towards the door. 'At least I'll still be in charge of something.'

'There's a good boy.'

CHAPTER TWENTY-EIGHT

None of Chilcott's pleas were accepted by DCI Foster. She had made her decision, and that was final. DC Deans had been provided with a detailed ordnance survey map of the area and all properties within a radius of three miles from where Travis Yardley was first located. It was a small area to search in the larger scheme of things, but it was a start.

The area was primarily rural. Hinton Charterhouse being a small ancient village of around five hundred inhabitants, give or take. A crossroads at its heart took drivers North towards Bath on the road where Travis Yardley was found – East in the direction of Freshford and the busy A36 commuter road – South towards Norton St Phillip, and West towards the small outlying village of Wellow.

Deans had spread the map out wide on a large double desk, scanning it closely with the tips of his fingers carefully brushing the paper's surface as he went.

'Come on,' Chilcott said. 'We haven't got time to fanny about with ordinance maps.'

Deans looked up at him but didn't answer.

'I don't want to be out there all night, and we haven't got the custody time to play with,' Chilcott continued.

'You do want to find them, don't you?' Deans said.

'It's a waste of time. It's pitch black out there, and we've already come up blank with house-to-house enquiries.'

'You obviously missed something then. Didn't you, sir?'

Chilcott was about to argue but stopped himself upon seeing DCI Foster observing them from across the room.

'How certain are you that you can find them?' Chilcott asked Deans, giving DCI Foster another look.

Deans blinked and looked away. 'Nothing in this life is certain.'

'So, then why are we bothering to try? We're wasting valuable time.'

'Because I said so,' Foster said, joining them at the table. 'This is my call. DC Deans is here to assist us. He is not here to be ridiculed or made to feel unwelcome. There are no guarantees you'll find the victims, but at least we're giving it a go. We're up against it, Robbie and time is against us.'

Chilcott rolled his head and grunted. 'Bring the map, if you must,' he said to Deans stomping off towards the exit. 'Just be quick about it.'

The journey from Bristol took Chilcott, DC Chiba and DC Deans through Keynsham, where Yardley was being housed, through the south-western fringes of Bath, and on towards Midford Valley and Hinton Charterhouse. It had been one of those early spring days that you wished you could bottle.

There was a promise of better things to come, but the atmosphere inside the car, like the outside now, was dark and cold. Chilcott hadn't spoken since taking the wheel, and Deans had made no attempt to change that. Penny Chiba, by contrast, did her best to engage Deans in small-talk, but that was all it was.

As they passed the spot where the ambulance picked up Yardley, Chilcott noticed Deans turn and look out of the window and back over his shoulder.

'Are you okay?' Chilcott asked him.

'Yeah. I'm fine, sir.'

'What was that?'

'What was what?'

'What were you looking at?'

Deans turned and faced Chilcott with a knowing look.

Chilcott whacked the steering wheel with irritation, his mind deep in thought and riddled with questions.

'So, like what happens?' Chilcott asked. 'I mean, how will you know if we find the crime scene?'

'I'll just know,' Deans said softly.

'But how? We can't see a thing out here.'

A small smile formed in the corner of Deans' mouth. 'It's hard to explain.'

They continued onwards with no other words spoken until they reached the first property on the edge of the village.

'Keep going,' Deans said. 'It isn't here.'

But instead, Chilcott brought the car to a halt at the side of the road.

'It isn't here,' Deans repeated, not taking his eyes from the windscreen.

Chilcott looked in the rear-view mirror at DC Chiba, who shrugged in response.

Without saying a word, Chilcott hit the accelerator and re-joined the road.

'Alright,' he said after another hundred metres or so. 'Tell me where we're going?'

'I don't know yet? Just keep going.'

'Do I keep going until you tell me to stop?'

Deans nodded and looked out through his side window.

Chilcott slowed on the approach to the four-way crossing in the heart of the village coming up ahead. A large van was now behind and only inches from his bumper.

'I'm going straight unless you tell me otherwise,' Chilcott said with his attention on the impatient driver behind them.

'Turn right,' Deans said. 'Turn right.'

Chilcott braked hard and immediately turned right at the junction, causing the driver behind to take evasive action with a loud, angry blast of the horn.

'Maybe give me a bit more notice next time,' Chilcott grumbled as he slowed the car on the much narrower country lane.

'Keep going,' Deans directed.

'Where to?'

Deans didn't answer. He was now straining against his seat belt, leaning forwards with anticipation.

There were no street lamps – just the light of Chilcott's full-beam lighting the thirty metres of twisting lane ahead of them.

'Wait, slow down,' Deans directed as they approached a high stone wall on their right-hand side. 'Slow down,' he said again.

Chilcott huffed and reluctantly brought the car's speed down to a walking pace.

In the passenger seat, Deans was far more animated than at any time before as he bobbed and strained to look ahead.

'Go in there,' he said as a break in the wall appeared on their right-hand side.

Chilcott indicated and slowly turned the car between two grey stone pillars adorned with dragon gargoyles in flight and aged by decades of protecting the property contained behind the high stone walls. He continued slowly, the long pea-gravel driveway crunching beneath the wheels. On either side of the driveway, well-groomed ornamental bushes sat positioned equally distanced from one another, and a string of old-style lanterns lit the way ahead and around a bend and out of sight.

Chilcott ground the car to a stop.

'Are you sure about this?' he asked Deans. 'It looks like we've just driven onto Lord and Lady Muck's country estate.'

'Keep going,' Deans replied, pulling against his seatbelt as he peered ahead through the windscreen.

'I hope you're right about this. I'm not dropping in the shit for you. I hope you realise that. This one is on you, son.'

Deans didn't respond, and soon they approached a large, imposing country manor building glowing a buttery yellow in the full beam of Chilcott's headlights.

Chilcott brought the car to a halt, well shy of the main entrance.

'You go,' he said to Deans and Chiba. 'I'll stay here and keep the engine running. I've got a feeling you're going to get a less than warm reception, and I don't want anything to do with it.'

Deans gave Chilcott a look and then stepped out of the car, and together with DC Chiba, they strode the fifty or so paces to the front door.

Chilcott killed the engine, dimmed the lights and took in the front of the property. A vehicle was protected beneath a full-sized frost jacket. Small mounds of leaves, twigs and debris were gathered on the sizeable front lawn, and a cast-iron table with two chairs was positioned beneath the spread of a majestic-looking blue cedar tree. Chilcott's shoulders slumped, and just at that moment the door opened to Deans and Chiba, and two elderly-looking residents engaged them in cautious conversation.

A couple of moments later, the detectives returned to the car.

'I hope you apologised to them. Poor old buggers. They probably haven't mixed with commoners for years.'

'Something's not right,' Deans said as if to himself, as much as anyone listening. He looked out into the darkness through the side windows.

'I'll tell you what's not right. Neither of them is dead. Well, they weren't until you just scared the living shit out of them? Probably keeling over with a heart attack as we speak—'

'What's that?' Deans said over the top of Chilcott's mutterings.

'What?'

'That track?'

Before Chilcott could answer, Deans was out of the car and approaching the front of the house again.

'Oh, for God's sake,' Chilcott groaned as he saw the disgruntled couple re-emerging at the front door. This time, Deans remained chatting to them for some minutes before returning at a pace.

'Well?' Chilcott asked.

'Go down that track, please. It leads to another property about half a mile away.'

'I'm not going down—'

'Just do it, sir. Please.'

Chilcott peered in the mirror, and Chiba gave him a non-committal shrug.

'Do they know who lives there?' he asked.

'Yes, they do.'

'Have they spoken to them or seen them since the weekend?'

'No. Neither of them.'

'Can they call them?'

'They tried while I was there. There wasn't an answer.'

Chilcott considered his next move.

'Do we know who lives there at least?'

Deans turned to Chilcott with determination in his face.

'It's an elderly mother and her daughter.'

Chilcott huffed loudly.

'Do we know if this one was covered by house-to-house?' he asked DC Chiba.

DC Chiba looked down at her notes.

'It doesn't look like it, sir.'

'Okay. I'll indulge you. But I'm not doing this all night. This is the last wild goose chase we're doing. Have you got that?'

They drove slowly along the tramlines of the soil and

stone track. A scruffy grass mound between the tyre treads suggested this wasn't a well-used path.

'Yes,' Deans said breathlessly. 'This is it.'

Up ahead, Chilcott could see the outline of a several farm buildings in the headlights. A wall-mounted lamp lit up an area in front of the main property.

As they got closer, Deans' breathing became increasingly laboured.

'Are you okay, son?' Chilcott asked him.

'They're here,' Deans breathed.

'Who are?'

Deans stared with wild eyes at Chilcott. 'The victims.'

Chilcott looked ahead, now paying more attention to his environment.

'Are you sure, son?' he asked. 'It doesn't scream of a crime scene. There's someone home. The lights are on.'

'Leave the car here,' Deans said, reaching for the door handle. 'We don't want to disturb the evidence.'

Chilcott stopped the car and gawped at the detective sitting next to him.

'You're serious, aren't you?'

'Are you coming?' Deans said, stepping out and walking with care in the direction of the farm buildings.

Chilcott caught himself looking in the mirror before catching DC Chiba staring back at him from the rear seats.

'Just wait until I see Julie,' Chilcott muttered. 'I'm not happy about this bullshit. I'm not happy about this at all.'

They both got out and made towards Deans, pacing headstrong towards the buildings.

'So, who are we about to scare the living daylights out of here then, Deans?' Chilcott asked.

'Mrs Betty Gilbert and her daughter Madeleine.'

'I'll leave you to do the talking, shall I?'

Deans stopped abruptly and held out an arm, stopping Chilcott and Chiba from walking any further.

In the unkempt hedgerow, just ahead of them, a flash of light from the headlamps reflected into their faces. There was a shiny object on the ground. Deans slowly approached and knelt.

'Can you grab a forensic flag, please,' he said, not taking his eyes from the object, which was mostly concealed by the foliage of the hedgerow.

'What have you found?' Chilcott asked him.

'Have you got any means of flagging this exhibit?' Deans asked.

'I brought the raid box,' DC Chiba said. 'It's in the boot of the car. There should be something in there.'

'Exhibit?' Chilcott stepped closer to Deans. 'What do you mean, exhibit?'

DC Chiba returned with a bunch of bright yellow plastic V-shaped stands commonly used by CSI to identify the locations of exhibits at crime scenes.

'Perfect, thanks,' Deans said, taking the top one from her. He placed the bright numbered flag near to the object. Ignoring Chilcott, he stood upright and walked towards the property, his head moving from left to right as if he was following someone's movements.

Chilcott leaned over and took a closer look at the flagged object. It appeared to be a kitchen knife. And there were red markings on the blade. He shot bolt upright and looked for Deans, who was already between the farm building and the closest barn.

Chilcott and Chiba jogged after him and caught up with Deans nearing an open side door to the main farm building.

'Do you think we should call out that we're the police,' DC Chiba said. 'Just in case someone is wondering who these strange people are on their front-drive?'

'It won't do any good,' Deans said, removing forensic shoe-overs and purple nitrile gloves from a side pocket of his jacket. 'Make sure you are forensically aware,' he said, pulling the protection over his shoes and hands.

Chilcott was panting from his short jog. He knew he was out of shape, but that was ridiculous. DC Chiba handed him shoe-overs and a pair of forensic gloves.

'I doubt we'll be needing these,' he said, sucking air back into his lungs.

'Put them on please, sir,' Deans instructed. 'I'm serious.'

'Bloody waste of time if you ask me,' Chilcott mumbled to himself as he struggled to pull the covers over his shoes. 'But who am I? I'm just the boss.'

Deans waited until they were ready and then took several careful steps towards the open door.

'Hello,' Chilcott called out loudly from behind Deans' back. 'There's no need to be alarmed. We are the police. We're conducting a welfare visit—' He stopped abruptly and stared open-mouthed at the open wooden door. The tell-tale signs of dried on blood hand marks smeared the door handle and frame.

He looked at Deans for a long second and then at Chiba. 'Right, switch on and watch where you're stepping.'

Splattered blood stains and foot marks continued on the kitchen flagstone flooring, and they continued on through, and then Deans stopped before the open inner doorway. In the darkened hallway ahead lay the silhouetted body of a female lying face down on the beige carpet.

As they tip-toed closer, a darkened circle of carpet framed the body.

'Oh, shit!' Chilcott said. 'We're going to have to check for a pulse.'

'She's dead,' Deans said, turning around and walking back towards the kitchen.

Chilcott flicked on the hallway light, and the full extent of the horror came into view. The victim's grey dressing gown was drenched in blood from behind and going from the size of the slick surrounding her; she had bled out on the carpet.

Chilcott knelt down to get a closer look at the victim's face. Her mouth was open, and her grey hair was dangling down over her face into the sticky pool of blood.

'Holy shit,' Chilcott breathed. 'She must be in her seventies.'

He looked at the floor and saw the bloody footprints go in both directions. He looked behind and realised Deans had gone.

'Stay here,' he said to DC Chiba. 'I'd better see where Deans is going?'

Deans was waiting for Chilcott next to a side entrance of the barn conversion closest to the main farm property.

'Be prepared,' Deans said.

'For what?'

Deans didn't answer and gently twisted the door handle, causing the latch to disengage. He gave the door a push with his fingers, and it arced wide and open. The unmistakable smell of death greeted them from inside, and they gave each other a look and stepped gingerly into the hallway.

'Where do you think the body is?' Chilcott asked Deans.

'She's in the main bedroom,' Deans said, continuing along the corridor.

CHAPTER TWENTY-NINE

A soft off-white light illuminated a section of the hallway outside of a fully-opened side door up ahead. The entire length of the hallway was adorned with framed family pictures on either side. Deans and Chilcott walked along the edge of the honey-coloured floorboards, as close to the side wall as they could get, so as not to disturb any footprints hidden by sight. They needn't have worried themselves too much, though, as deep red scuffs and stains led away from the open doorway towards them in a close and uniformed pattern.

'He didn't run,' Chilcott commented, looking down at visible dried footprints. 'He wasn't in any hurry to get away.'

'This was the first victim,' Deans said. 'She was what he was really after.'

They followed the macabre trail, Deans at the front, and then he stopped cold at the entrance to the open bedroom doorway.

'Oh, dear God,' Chilcott choked and covered his mouth as he came alongside Deans. 'Oh, Jesus, no!'

Deans didn't speak. He stood utterly still, his eyes scoping the room.

'I think we can safely say we don't need to find a pulse from this one,' Chilcott said, coughing away the acrid taste of death.

Deans stepped forwards into the room. His head was now moving as if watching someone ahead of him.

'What is it?' Chilcott asked him.

Deans stepped slowly towards a pile of clothes discarded on the floor.

'We'll need a full CSI team,' Deans said. 'Get Nathan Parsons – he's the best man for the job.'

'Nathan works for us anyway,' Chilcott said. 'He's been managing forensics at my team for the past fifteen months.'

'Tell him to bring plenty of helpers,' Deans said, not taking his eyes away from the gory scene.

Chilcott stepped cautiously into the room. He looked around briefly before his eyes fell upon his victim.

She was dangling.

Her arms were out to the side and her wrists tied to the end crossbar of the four-poster bed. Her feet suspended off the ground, limp, mannequin-like, except they were caked in crimson red sticky blood. The smell was appalling. Chilcott had been to the scenes of many bloody deaths, but this one was something else. Mainly because the victim had been opened up from below the chin right down to her navel – her organs, or what was left of them, were exposed with her intestines hanging down between her legs in a ropey pile on the floor.

She'd been hanging there for four days, slowly cooking beside the heat of an oil-filled radiator that was so hot,

Chilcott could feel the baking heat from where he was standing.

Extreme heat and dead bodies don't mix, and flies were buzzing around their heads and pitching on their skin. Chilcott hated flies – the disgusting, shit-eating, germ-spreading critters.

'I'll call it in,' he said from behind a pocket handkerchief as he batted more flies away with his free hand.

Deans nodded, not taking his eyes away from the mutilated victim.

Chilcott stepped outside into the cool, fresh air and walked around to the front of the farmhouse where he would not be seen by either DC Chiba or DC Deans, should they emerge outside. He panted and spluttered, trying to shake the growing sensation of nausea.

He stayed there for a few minutes, sucking in fresh air through his nostrils, cleansing his lungs. But as he did his best to rid the smell, he couldn't work out what disturbed him most – the shocking crime scene or the fact Detective Deans had brought him directly to it.

When he returned to the bedroom, Deans was crouched against the back wall, his hands clutching his face, and he was mumbling incoherently beneath his breath.

'Deans. Are you okay, son?' Chilcott asked him.

Deans looked up at him. His eyes were reddened and haunted. 'Great again…' he mumbled. 'Great again…'

'Yeah, okay. I'll give you credit for finding this place, but are you okay?' Chilcott repeated.

Deans didn't speak and returned his face to his sweaty palms, rocking gently back and forth.

'I've got four marked units coming. All available CSI crews, including Nathan Parsons. A specialist search team and the DCI with a couple more troops from the office. I've asked comms to notify the coroner's officer, but I expect we'll be here for some time with the bodies in-situ as forensics do their thing with the victims.'

Chilcott stepped as close to the body as he dared without contaminating the scene. 'I just can't get my head around why he would do this?' he said. 'Why he would cause this much damage?'

'She was dead before he tied her up and cut her open,' Deans said into his lap. 'Look up at the ceiling above the bed.'

Chilcott did as suggested and saw the tell-tale crimson splatter pattern of a frenzied knife attack. Arcs of blood flicked high onto the ceiling and rear wall as the attacker repeatedly lunged with the blade.

'The bed is soaked through,' Deans said. 'He killed her where she lay.'

He peered up and pointed to the corpse dangling from the bedposts.

'*That...*' he said. 'That is a display of his dominance. A *fuck you* message.'

'A fuck you message to who – us?'

'Maybe?'

Chilcott asked as he studied the perplexing detective leaning against the wall.

'Are you sure you're okay?'

'Yeah. I'll be alright. Thanks.'

'Why don't you go outside and get some air as we wait for the troops to arrive.'

Chilcott gestured with his head towards the victim. 'She isn't going anywhere.'

Deans stood up, straightening his back. Head bowed, he walked out of the door without so much as a second glance at the victim.

CHAPTER THIRTY

'Tell them to kill the bloody sirens,' Chilcott shouted down the radio to comms as he heard the distant wailing of multiple police vehicles approaching their location. 'Jesus Christ, talk about drawing attention to yourself,' he said to Deans, who was sitting on a sturdy garden bench in front of the farmhouse, his head resting against the external stone wall, and his eyes tightly bunched.

Chilcott imagined the old girl inside enjoying the first signs of spring from this very bench – South-facing if he wasn't mistaken. On either side, vast ornamental pots contained the young shoots of recently-planted shrubs and plants.

It was a bitterly cold night, and the air was crisp with the menace of another sharp frost. *Not good for the younglings,* Chilcott thought. *Still, what does that matter now?*

DC Chiba was now also outside. She'd been alone with the older body inside the farm for the last twenty-five minutes, and she needed some air.

'I'm going to meet the marked units at the front gate,'

Chilcott said. 'They'll never find this place in the dark. Can you come with me? I just need to speak to Lord and Lady Muck and make sure they don't have a nose around down here, or we'll have four bloody bodies to contend with.

'No problem. It has done us a favour, sir, finding this scene at night. Hopefully, we should get our work done without the media filming every move we make.'

'Never underestimate the newshounds, Penny. They'll be here. Don't you doubt it.'

DC Chiba smiled thinly at Deans even though his eyes were still firmly closed. 'Will you be alright here, Andy? We won't be long.'

Deans bobbed his head but kept his eyelids shut.

Chilcott gave Deans a considered look. 'Come on,' he said to Chiba. 'We best get ourselves up there.'

They jumped in the car, and as they bounced back out along the rough, bumpy track, Chilcott looked back in the rear-view mirror. Deans was illuminated by a bright V-shaped shaft of light from the outside flood lamp.

Returning to the grand old manor house, as DC Chiba drove back along the driveway to intercept the incoming police vehicles, Chilcott tapped on the large wooden door. He was met by the elderly lady of the residence.

'I'm very sorry to trouble you again, madam. But I'm with the police officer who spoke to you earlier.'

'Are you still here?'

'I'm afraid so. And I need to make you aware that you will be seeing a lot of police activity for several hours and probably through tomorrow or longer.'

The lady put a hand to mouth and emitted a startled, 'Oh.'

'I'm afraid we have come across a serious crime scene at your neighbour's property, and we will be closing the road. So, if you need to go anywhere tonight—'

'Is Betty okay?'

'I'm afraid I can't go into any details at the moment... uh, but would you happen to know the full names of the people who live along the lane from you?'

'Isn't Madeleine there? Can she not help you?'

'I'm afraid there's no one there who can assist us right now.'

'Well, Betty lives in the original farmhouse, and her daughter, Madeleine, lives in one of the converted out-buildings.'

'And their surname please?' Chilcott asked scribbling the details in his daybook. Deans had already told him but he wasn't paying much attention then. That had all changed now.

'Gilbert. I've known Betty for almost fifty years and her daughter for all of her life.'

Chilcott looked up at the lady. 'Does anyone else live or frequent the property? Were either of them married or partnered?'

'No. David died some time ago. That was Betty's husband. And Madeleine is dedicated to her mother – God bless her. Shall I come down and talk to them – make sure they're alright?'

'No. No, please. Please, there is no need to come down to the farm. As I say, this is a serious police investigation, and I'd respectfully request that you remain indoors for now.'

'Oh.'

'I'm sorry to be blunt, but we need space to conduct our enquiries. Uh, just one thing. Do you have CCTV here at all?'

'No, of course not. Nothing ever happens here to warrant the extravagant cost of CCTV.'

'Of course,' he smiled, but he knew deep down that once news broke of the killings, that would be one of the first things the local residents would rush out to buy.

Within the half-hour, the farm was heaving with police and CSI activity. A double-crewed unit was at the main gate, creating an outer perimeter. An officer was with the elderly couple from the mansion, making sure they weren't too alarmed, and the DCI in company with two more detectives and the specialist search team were making good ground to the crime scene.

'How are you feeling?' Chilcott asked Deans when they had a moment to themselves.

Deans inclined his head as he looked at Chilcott. 'You know…'

'Now's not the time, son. But I need to talk to you about all of… *this*.'

Deans looked away. 'I know.'

'I just can't—'

'Talk to me later, boss,' Deans said. 'Let's just get this sorted here, and we'll talk when we're back at the nick.'

CHAPTER THIRTY-ONE

Two hours later, police activity was in full swing. CSI had evidenced the bodies as they were found, the victims had been removed to the mortuary and search team officers were scouring the surroundings for signs of further evidence. However, Chilcott suspected Yardley hadn't attempted to conceal anything. DCI Foster was calling the shots from the ground but would return to the custody centre along with Chilcott as a further wave of detectives continued to arrive from Bath's Falcon Road CID and the major crime team in Bristol.

A news broadcasting helicopter had recently appeared overhead, but Chilcott was confident they had got the bodies away before any cameras were pointed in their direction. The media weren't stupid though, and Chilcott knew operations on this scale were almost unheard of in these parts, and as such, the news reporters would be all over it like a prickly rash, and Foster had already called DI Chowdhury and put him on standby to knock up a press release for the cameras. Even though it was late, the area's local residents would also be aware that something major was happening, and the gossip would be starting like wildfire.

As they drove back towards the custody centre in Keynsham, Chilcott was unusually quiet in the front passenger seat.

'Has that shaken you?' Foster asked him.

'Yeah. Yeah, it has. It's not every day we have to see something as gruesome as that.'

'I know. You've done a good job, you and Deans.'

Chilcott sighed. 'Yeah… Deans…'

Foster looked over at him as she drove.

'Something on your mind?' she asked.

Chilcott raised his brows as far they could reach.

'You could say that.'

'Well, go on then. It's just the two of us.'

Chilcott scratched the back of his head.

'Do you believe all that stuff?'

'What stuff?'

'That he can visualise crime scenes and that sort of stuff?'

'He's just proven it, hasn't he?'

'Well, yeah… but…'

'There is no but, Robbie. He has a gift that none of us will ever understand. We must thank our lucky stars that he's one of us, and we can utilise his skills, as we've seen today.'

Chilcott pinched his bottom lip between his teeth as he struggled to comprehend just exactly what had happened today and what he had witnessed Deans do in the last six hours.

'Don't try to understand it, Rob. I don't,' Foster said as she took a right turn at the next junction.

Chilcott sighed deeply. 'Where is he now?'

'I sent him back to his station. He wasn't looking too good.'

'I know. But Deans thinks quite a lot of himself, don't you think? He was bigging himself up like anything at the scene.'

'And for a good reason,' Foster smiled.

Chilcott grunted, and they continued for two further miles without another word spoken, and then Chilcott said what was playing on his mind.

'Do you think we should let him loose on Yardley?'

'Who?' Foster asked like she didn't know what was going on in Chilcott's mind.

'DC Deans. Do you think we should allow Deans to meet Yardley? He... he...'

'He may be of use to us?'

'Exactly.'

'I don't see why not. Yardley's forensic evidence was gathered long before you or Deans went to the scene. So, there would be no question of cross-contamination defences in court.'

'I wasn't thinking of that.'

'I know what you were thinking.'

'It's a game-changer. To have someone like that, who does... *that*. It's mind-boggling.'

'I agree.' Foster half-smiled.

Chilcott raked the top of his head with long scrapes as he thought further.

'Do you think we can trust him?' he asked. 'Looking at him today, it was like he was haunted or something.'

Foster glanced wearily at her DI. 'From what I've heard, that's probably not too far from the mark.'

'How well do you know him?'

'I don't.'

'Okay then. How much do you know about him?'

'I know enough not to ask him about what happened.' Foster pulled a troubled face and looked at herself in the mirror.

Chilcott didn't respond.

'I wasn't involved in the case,' Foster continued after a pregnant silence. 'But I watched it unfold, along with pretty much everyone else who had a TV at the time.'

Chilcott acknowledged the comment. He saw the media frenzy associated with Andy Deans those twenty-something months before. He had never met Deans until the day he came to the office. Still, he thought the world's cameras brought unnecessary attention to the constabulary and created an unsettling environment for the team.

'I respect the fact that Deans is still in the job. That he has the strength and desire to continue.'

'Yeah,' Chilcott agreed.

'So, I think it would be to our advantage to have Deans on board in whatever capacity he can help us. I mean, just look at today. How long would it have taken for us to discover that crime scene without his input?'

Chilcott stared out of his side window. 'I know,' he said. 'It's bonkers. It's truly bonkers.'

'I say we don't do anything more with Deans tonight.

He has already displayed that he's invested in the investigation. He can't walk away now.'

'So, what do we do?'

'I'll call him in the morning. I'll ask him if he has any further information. Did you see his face at the scene?'

'Yeah. It was like he had just witnessed the murders first-hand.'

'We'll wait for CSI to get some crime scene images to us, and then we'll hit Yardley with another interview tonight.' She looked at the time on the dashboard. 'We need to be in a position to charge ASAP. I don't want us to run out of custody time.'

CHAPTER THIRTY-TWO

'What's the plan?' the custody sergeant asked Chilcott and Foster, calling them across to the charge desk.

'We've just come from the crime scene,' Foster said. 'It's a bloody mess.'

'So I heard.'

'Who from?' Chilcott asked.

The custody sergeant gestured towards a door behind him, and Chilcott and Foster walked through.

DC Andy Deans was seated at the desk.

'I thought I told you to go back to your station.'

'I thought I'd be more help here, Ma'am.'

Foster turned to Chilcott with a smug expression of vindication.

'Well then, as you're here,' Chilcott said. 'Perhaps you could talk us through what happened earlier?'

Deans ran a hand behind his head and massaged an area behind his left ear.

'I mean, how did you know where to go for starters?'

'I felt it.'

'How?'

Deans' eyes glazed, and he looked away.

'You don't have to tell us.'

'Yes – you do,' Chilcott spoke over his boss. 'I need to understand how you knew that stuff, how you were able to take us there. And how you knew the victim was in the bedroom? At some point, I'm going to have to justify to a judge how we followed a non-existent chain of evidence to lead us to that farmhouse.'

Deans nodded, looking down to his feet.

'I don't ask for any of this,' he said. 'But it's something I have to live with.'

He stood up from his seat and approached Chilcott square on.

'I saw the crime through the eyes of the victim. I saw him straddle her. I saw the blade in his hands. And I felt the searing pain.' His voice trailed away.

'I just don't understand how?'

'We don't need to understand, Robbie. Let's just be thankful we were able to find them.'

Chilcott groaned loudly, battling with his instincts.

'You said you saw him. Was it Yardley?' he asked Deans.

'Yes. I've seen his website image.'

'Okay. We need to wait for the crime scene images to come through. It shouldn't be long now. And then we'll re-interview Yardley. I want you in there with me.'

Deans closed his eyes and sank back down to his chair.

'I know.'

. . .

Yardley was a gibbering wreck of a man and in complete contrast to his previous demeanour. Chilcott slid five crime scene images across the table towards him – one being the external farm buildings from just along the stone track. One of the open kitchen door smeared with dried blood. One photograph of the older victim lying face down in the hallway in a pool of her own blood. One at the entrance to the outbuilding, and finally one of the mutilated body of the younger victim as she hung by her wrists from the bedpost crossbar. In the lower corner of the photograph, a pile of men's clothing was at the foot of the bed.

Yardley drew away, his face contorted in horror.

'I'm going to be sick. I'm going to be sick,' Yardley said, convulsing into his hands.

'Get a bucket,' Chilcott called out.

Moments later, a detention officer entered the room with a plastic waste paper bin.

No sooner had Yardley seen the bucket than his head was deep inside, vomiting violently.

'Thank you,' his solicitor said. 'My client has seen those images.'

Chilcott pulled them back towards him but kept them in view on the table.

'Tell me what you're thinking,' Chilcott asked Yardley.

'I… I can't…' Yardley cried.

Chilcott turned to Deans, who was looking keenly at the man before them.

'We found a wallet with bank cards in your name,' Chilcott said. 'It was in the back pocket of a pair of jeans. The jeans on the floor next to first victim's bed.' He nudged the image back towards Yardley. 'Those jeans.'

Yardley didn't speak. His mouth was quivering.

'A phone was also in the trouser pocket. It is being analysed as we speak, and we have reason to believe it is your phone.'

Chilcott waited another ten seconds.

'The clothes found in the bedroom match the clothes you were wearing that night, as can be seen on CCTV that we've recovered from various sources. Not only that, we are cross-matching the victims' blood to the blood found on your body.'

'My client will not be answering any questions at this time.'

Chilcott looked at Mr Wilson but continued speaking. 'Your prints are all over a bloody kitchen knife found at the scene. A knife we believe you used to inflict fatal injuries to both victims.'

Yardley blubbered incoherently.

'Why did you do it, son?'

Yardley didn't reply.

Chilcott shook his head. 'Think about your family. Think about the effect this will have on your girls.'

Yardley dropped his hands away from his face.

'Wh…what?'

'Your actions have far-reaching implications beyond this table.'

'Why would you mention my girls?' Yardley said, wiping his eyes with the back of his hands. 'Why would you bring them up?'

Chilcott interlocked his fingers and stared at his suspect.

'Because it's just not about you. You've just ruined the lives of everyone who loves you.'

Yardley's face tightened, and his eyes narrowed. 'My girls are dead.'

Chilcott stopped himself and glowered at Yardley.

'You what?' he said.

'My girls died three years ago,' Yardley wept. 'And not a single day goes by when I don't think about them.'

Mr Wilson leaned across and touched Yardley's arm. 'Don't say anymore,' he encouraged gently. 'You don't need to talk about any of this.'

Chilcott turned sideways to Deans, staring with fixated intent at Yardley as he spoke.

'I don't understand?' Chilcott said. 'We have been speaking to your ex-wife. She told us she was arranging their schooling while she was assisting us here.'

Yardley gazed between Chilcott and Deans. His face was crushed with emotion. 'I should have been there,' he muttered.

'Where? Where should you have been?'

'At the house.'

'With your two daughters?'

'Yes.'

'Amelia and Lily-Belle?'

'Yes.'

The mere mention of their names brought tears to his eyes.

'Three years ago, you say?'

Yardley stared vacantly at the table. Strands of mucus clung to his lips.

Deans turned to Chilcott and nodded.

'I'm sorry…' Chilcott said, scratching the side of his

face. 'But we have spoken to your wife today, and she has told us your two girls are very much alive.'

Yardley rocked back in his seat and rolled his head like he was trying to forget a nightmare.

'She can't accept it,' he said. 'She says I am to blame.'

'For their deaths?'

'Yes…'

'They all died,' Deans said faintly. 'Not just your girls.'

Chilcott stared at him. 'Sorry. What did you just say?'

'They all died in a house fire – didn't they, Mr Yardley.'

Yardley dipped his head, and an outpouring of emotion overcame him.

'They were at their grandparents' house in Dundee. I should have been there, but I was meeting with a local theatre company when…'

'When what?'

'I should have been there to save them…' Yardley wailed, breaking down into a heap on the table. 'All of them.'

As Yardley cried, Chilcott stared open-mouthed at his colleague.

'It's not your fault,' Deans said, leaning forwards and touching Yardley's arm.

'It is my fault,' Yardley howled. 'I was selfish and could only think about myself. And now, look at me…' He peered at Deans with fractured eyes.

'There was no chance for them,' Deans said.

Chilcott gawped at Deans.

'She has blamed me ever since,' Yardley sobbed.

'Were the others your parents?'

'No… they were Georgia's parents. They died too.'

Chilcott coughed twice to get Deans' attention. 'Right, I think that's enough of this conversation.'

He stared at Deans, struggling to comprehend what was happening. Was Yardley using his acting skills to buy sympathy? And what did Deans think he was doing?'

'You had better go back to your cell while we seek advice from the Crown Prosecution Service,' Chilcott said.

'Will that be tonight?' the solicitor asked, looking at his watch.

'Yes. It will.'

The solicitor looked at his watch again. 'Fine. There's no point in me going home then, is there. I'll remain with my client for the time being. You've got my mobile number. Give me a call the moment you have a charging decision.'

Chilcott gave him a tight-lipped smile. 'You'll be the first to know.'

CHAPTER THIRTY-THREE

Chilcott gawped at DC Deans, who was returning to the small rest area with a polystyrene black coffee cradled between his hands.

'What was that?' Chilcott asked him.

Deans took a sip of coffee and sat on the edge of the faux leather sofa.

'What?'

'That stuff about his girls dying in a house fire.'

'You might want to check it out, sir,' Deans said, taking another loud slurp.

'Are you saying I might want to check it out, or are you telling me to check it out?'

Deans shrugged, looking at Chilcott through the steam of the hot drink.

'I know what I'd do,' he said.

'We've already checked him out. He's clean. No police reports. No nothing.'

'You checked out Travis Yardley.' Deans left his eyes on Chilcott.

Chilcott shuffled his feet and scratched the side of his head. 'It's a bit of an own goal if his kids and in-laws are still alive, don't you think?'

'One way to find out.'

Chilcott smiled.

'I'm still trying to figure out if I like you or not?' he said, aiming a crooked finger in Deans' direction.

Deans brought the beaker to his lips but didn't reply.

Chilcott cleared the back of his throat and pondered his thoughts for an instant.

'I never got the chance to say I'm sorry... for—'

'You don't have to be sorry for anything.'

Chilcott scratched the lobe of his ear. 'I saw the news at the time,' he said. 'It was everywhere.'

Deans nodded.

'That must have been hard for you? All that media attention. When you were trying to process the shock of it all and deal with the emotion of your loss.'

'It was. And it still is.'

Chilcott pondered his thoughts. 'I don't know if I could have coped with that myself. Fair play.'

He noticed Deans glazing over.

Chilcott looked away awkwardly and coughed behind closed lips.

'I appreciate it must be difficult to talk about what happened.'

'I don't have a problem talking about it.' Deans shrugged and pulled a face. 'Everyone else, on the other hand...'

Chilcott shook his head. 'What you did today... how you were able to find that crime scene. It just... I don't know?'

'It's horrific,' Deans said. 'It is horrific.'

Chilcott clutched his chin and turned around in a tight circle as he thought about it further.

'I mean… you saw that? You literally saw that crime scene in your dream?'

Deans dropped his head and played with the half beaker of coffee between his hands.

'Why you?' Chilcott asked delicately after an uncomfortable thirty seconds of silence.

'I guess I'm lucky, sir,' Deans said, still looking down to his beaker.

'Is that irony?'

Deans looked up and half-smiled. 'I'm still trying to figure that question out for myself.'

'Okay then. Why this crime – why did you choose to envisage this particular crime?'

'I didn't. It chose me.'

'I don't understand?' Chilcott walked over to Deans and sat down on the arm of the sofa alongside him.

'This gift that you have – call it what you will—'

'I call it a bloody burden.'

Chilcott glanced momentarily at his younger colleague.

'Well then, this burden. When did it all begin?'

Deans pinched the bridge of his nose and then wiped his hand down across his eyes and face.

'It began when I experienced true loss.' He looked Chilcott square in the eyes. 'I didn't want it. I didn't need it. But it saddled me, and now I wear it like it's a part of me.'

'Wow!'

'It is also a comfort for me.'

'How so?' Chilcott asked, looking deeply into Deans' wetting eyes.

'Because I'm closest when it happens.'

Chilcott inclined his head. 'Did you ever consider giving up?'

Deans turned away. 'Every day.'

Chilcott sniffed. 'Well, son. I'm pleased you didn't today.' He patted Deans on the knee and hauled himself back to his feet.

'So, I guess we now need to find proof of a couple of dead kids and their grandparents to show that our prime suspect is somehow innocent in all of this?'

'He's not innocent. But it's not what it seems. He absolutely believes what he is saying in there. Travis Yardley has no idea what happened to those women. But Jesse Garcia did.'

'That's what I feared. Come on, drink up – we've got a long night ahead of us.'

When they arrived back at the major crime offices, the team of detectives were still working hard at it. The exhibits had come in from the crime scene, and the officers were logging each of the items onto the detained property system.

One exhibit caught Chilcott's eye, and he walked across to DC McEwan to take a closer look.

'I've got one of those myself,' he said to McEwan.

'Ten quid for one of these, boss. Must be mad paying that.'

'I got mine for free from my new friend at the theatre.

Have you looked through it?' Chilcott said, lifting the exhibit bag from the table.

'No, boss. I'm more of a *Netflix* kind of bloke.'

The security bag wasn't sealed, and Chilcott pulled on a pair of forensic gloves before gently removing the theatre programme from the clear plastic bag. He considered the outside covers for a second before flicking his way through the familiar pages.

'What've you got there?' DC Deans asked over the top of Chilcott's shoulder.

'It's a theatre programme from Saturday night. It lists all the actors, and some of them have a write-up. Hold on; I'll show you Yardley's.'

Chilcott thumbed his way through a couple more pages and then spread the double pages carefully on top of the forensic bag.

'What a smarmy git,' DC McEwan said. 'What has he written there?' He leaned forwards and muttered the words to himself. 'He thinks he's God's bloody gift.'

'Wait,' Deans said abruptly. 'Look at the signature.'

Chilcott and McEwan peered closer.

'What?' McEwan asked. 'What's the problem?'

'He's signed it, *Travis Yardley*.'

CHAPTER THIRTY-FOUR

'So, what we've got here is one of two things; either, he has been playing us this entire time, and he's been acting, or he wasn't hypnotised when he signed that programme. Either way, it's not what I wanted to be dealing with at this late stage of the job,' Chilcott said.

'How can we find out?' McEwan asked.

Chilcott chewed the inside of his cheek and squinted. 'The CCTV.'

'Which CCTV, boss?' McEwan asked.

Chilcott rushed over to DC Fowler's desk with McEwan and Deans following close behind.

'Amy, have you got that CCTV to hand from the theatre side door?'

'Just give me a second, sir,' she said, clicking away pages on her screen and bringing up the CCTV software.

'What do you need, sir?'

'Show me that footage again when Yardley comes out from the theatre. The first time we see him.'

DC Fowler checked through her timeline and dragged the search bar to 10:21 p.m. 'Here we go, sir.'

She pressed play, and all four of them crowded the screen.

'There he is,' Chilcott said to McEwan and Deans. 'So, we see a few actors chatting to fans, and then this female comes into shot here.' He tapped the screen.

'That's the victim,' Deans said.

'Yes. That's our victim. Now watch.'

They viewed the screen in silence as Yardley interacted with the female for half a minute before being bumped and crowded away by another fan.

'I think I'm in the wrong job?' McEwan commented with a sarcastic laugh.

'So do I,' Chilcott answered, giving his DC a playful wink.

'I mean… is he all that? Look at those women fighting over him?' McEwan continued.

'He's an actor,' DC Fowler said. 'Perhaps you're in the wrong job if you want a profession for getting laid.'

'Nah,' Chilcott said. 'McEwan could be a professional footballer and still not get his leg over.'

The short clip finished, and they all stood upright.

'Any observations, apart from McEwan's virginity?' Chilcott asked.

'He wasn't exactly chivalrous towards that poor woman,' DC Fowler said.

'No, he wasn't,' Chilcott mused.

'I mean, I know he went on to slaughter her, but that was a bit cold,' DC Fowler went on.

'Yes, it was.'

Chilcott glanced back towards McEwan's desk and the theatre programme.

'Just show me that all again,' he said to DC Fowler.

They quietly watched it through for a second time. Chilcott's mind was working overtime.

'Who has the mobile phone?' he called out to the room of detectives.

'I did, sir, but it's in detained property now,' DC Chiba said.

'Has it been analysed yet?'

'Yes, sir.'

'Were there any messages to corroborate what the hypnotist has said?'

'Yes, sir.'

Chilcott walked to the rear desk where Penny Chiba was engrossed in her computer monitor.

'Got the details have you, Pen?'

She handed him a printout of call transactions from Yardley's phone. He looked through the times for Saturday night and stopped with his finger on an incoming voicemail. He looked closer; *10:13 p.m.*

'Do we know if this answerphone message was listened to?' he asked Chiba, showing her the data entry of interest.

'Yes, that one was listened to, sir. But three unanswered messages were waiting on the home screen of the phone.'

Chilcott scratched the top of his head, feeling suddenly hot.

. . .

DCI Foster's tired eyes skipped around Chilcott's face. Her lips were tight and dry. They were alone in her office, and the door was closed to interruptions. She wouldn't usually be in the office at nearly midnight, but these were extraordinary times and extraordinary times called for exceptional circumstances.

'If he wasn't hypnotised when he signed that theatre programme, do we believe he has been acting all this time? Is that even possible?'

'It's possible, but I think it is very unlikely,' Chilcott replied. 'It has been like having two different people in the cells.'

'But he is an actor.'

'He is and not a very good one unless he's hypnotised. Either way we look at it, he's been hypnotised while he's been with us in custody.'

'We know the hypnotist's message was listened to, but what we can't say is at what time, where or by whom?'

Chilcott pulled a face. 'True.'

'He could have listened to that at any point before leaving his belongings at the farmhouse.'

'Yes, but we have three more unanswered messages that he hasn't heard because they were waiting on the homepage of his phone.'

'What times were they?'

'The earliest was ten twenty-five. That's only twelve minutes after the listened-to message from the hypnotist. The other two came within a thirty-minute duration.'

'Okay,' Foster said, standing up. 'So, we think Yardley listened to the first message we have, but not the next three that followed in a thirty-odd-minute timespan, the second of which was only thirteen minutes after the first.'

'Something like that.'

'Follow me,' she said, making for the door.

She walked with Chilcott to the incident board and the timeline of events. She took a green marker pen and drew a vertical line just before the entry showing Yardley departing from the side exit of the theatre, and she scribbled *10:13* above it. She then drew a vertical dotted line through the period of time that Yardley could be seen outside on the CCTV, and above it, she wrote *Travis Yardley*. She then drew a second solid line just after the dotted line and wrote, *Unanswered voicemail @ 10:25*. She took a couple of steps back and looked at her work before stepping forward and ringing the twelve-minute space with a fat, double circle.

'There,' she said, banging the marker board with the end of the pen. 'Let's assume – because that's all we have – that Travis Yardley listened to the ten-thirteen voicemail from the hypnotist at some point after ten-thirteen and before ten twenty-one when we see him exiting the theatre. That gives us a window of exactly eight minutes for Yardley to come out of his hypnotic state. How long does the hypnotist's message last to bring him out of his trance?'

'Amy?' Chilcott called out to DC Fowler. 'How long is that message from the hypnotist that has been listened to?'

DC Fowler looked at her notes. 'Three minutes, twenty-nine seconds, sir.'

'Giving us around four and half minutes,' Foster said, looking up at the timeline. 'Something happened in those four and half minutes – potentially – to put Travis Yardley back under. But what?'

Chilcott stepped forward, taking the pen from DCI Foster's hand and laying it flat in the gulley of the marker board.

'Come with me, Julie. We should have all of those minutes captured on the CCTV camera footage.'

CHAPTER THIRTY-FIVE

They were in the High-Tech Crime office with its large TV monitor and sophisticated tracking systems. DC Fowler had loaded the CCTV, and together with Chilcott, Foster, McEwan and Deans, they were glued to the screen.

The window of opportunity was so small the slightest occurrence could mean the difference between success and failure of the case.

'Play that part again,' DCI Foster said to Fowler, who toggled the timer back thirty seconds.

They watched again.

'Who is that?' Foster asked.

'Just some groupie,' Chilcott said.

'Zoom in,' Foster requested.

DC Fowler increased the zoom, and they watched again.

'Where does that female come from?' Foster asked.

'From the others,' Chilcott said.

'No. She's come from the wrong angle. Watch again.'

Foster signalled for DC Fowler to play it again.

'See. She comes from behind and barges our victim out of the way.'

'What, you think that was deliberate?'

'Look again.'

They all watched for a fifth time as the woman shouldered Madeleine off balance and immediately placed her arm around the back of Travis Yardley's shoulder with her mobile phone primed and ready to take a selfie.

Chilcott scratched the back of his neck.

'To be fair,' he said, 'she does seem to make a beeline straight for our victim.'

'But look at him afterwards. Look at how he's standing,' Foster said.

'We made comments earlier that it was a bit bloody rude of him not to help our victim up.'

Foster turned to face them all. 'Ask yourselves why?'

She turned back to the screen. 'Have we got a facial shot of this selfie woman?'

'No, just the back of her hood, Ma'am.'

'What about the other cameras?'

'We didn't track her movements. I should imagine one of the cameras will pick her up.'

'Anyway,' Foster said. 'What words did the hypnotist use to put Yardley under? There must be some sort of sequence?'

'He said it's the tone of the voice that counts.'

'You didn't ask him?' Foster asked Chilcott.

'Not exactly, no.'

She looked at her watch. 'Sean, go out and call the hypnotist. Apologise for the time and all that, but find out what he says to put Yardley under, would you, please. Are we talking minutes or seconds here?'

'Yes, Ma'am,' McEwan said and dashed out of the room.

'Can we zoom closer into the phone?' DC Deans asked.

'Which phone, son?'

'The selfie.'

DC Fowler pulled a face and twiddled with the controls making the screen more pixilated.

'If we can't see her face directly on the CCTV, then maybe we'll be able to make it out from her phone screen? Deans said.

'This isn't MI-bloody-six, son.'

'No, I like it,' Foster said. 'Good thinking, Andy.'

They all peered closer, but the screen pixels were so grainy there was no chance of making anything out.

'If you squint,' DC Fowler said, 'you can only see one person.'

In unison, they all squinted at the screen.

'Oh, yeah,' Chilcott said. 'But the background is a solid bright colour.'

He looked over at DCI Foster as DC McEwan returned to the room.

'All right,' McEwan said. 'It's a bit of a weird one, but I've got what he said to put Travis Yardley into a hypnotic trance.'

They all turned to face McEwan.

'Go on,' DCI Foster said. 'Don't keep us guessing.'

McEwan began to laugh. 'I think he must have a good sense of humour.'

'Just bloody tell us what he said, will you,' Chilcott said.

'Okay… ready?'

'Ready to give you a belt around the ear.'

'Sorry, boss. Okay. Here it is… *Make Travis great again.* See what he's done there? It's like the Presidential elections all over again.'

Chilcott's face dropped like a clapped-out old washing machine tumbling off a hundred-foot cliff edge.

'What did you just say?'

'Which bit, boss? The Presidency…?'

Chilcott turned to Foster, his face fuelled with rage.

'I've heard that before,' he said, storming out of the room. 'In my bloody interview room.'

CHAPTER THIRTY-SIX

Chilcott was back on the phone to the hypnotist within seconds and re-affirmed what McEwan had just told them.

'Have you ever met Travis Yardley's wife?' Chilcott asked him.

'Yes, plenty of times.'

'In what capacity?'

'I'm afraid I can't share client privileges with you. I'm so sorry.'

'You've just told me enough; she was a patient. How long ago – three years by any chance?'

'Uh…'

'Was she ever with Travis when he was being hypnotised?'

'I, uh… I can't…'

'Listen,' Chilcott snarled. 'I'm asking you nicely, but that can all change just as quickly as I wish. We can do this from a police interview room if you'd prefer? I'm still figuring out if you are complicit in some way.'

'Uh… I'm really uncomfortable with this,' the hypnotist spluttered.

'Let me tell you what *is* uncomfortable; a five-centimetre-thick mattress, which is what you'll be sleeping on unless you start coughing up the info, mate.'

'Um, um… yes. Yes, she was with him on occasions.'

'She saw and heard you give the treatments?'

'Uh… she did, yes.'

'How many times?'

'I couldn't say.'

'But she heard enough to know what puts Travis Yardley into a hypnotic trance?'

'Y—ess.'

'Could she do it herself?'

'Um…'

'Could she do what you do to put him into a hypnotic state?'

'No.'

Chilcott frowned. 'No?'

'No… but she wouldn't have to.'

'And why might that be?'

'Because she has a recording of my treatment. They used it to great effect when they were travelling together with the theatre group.'

'She was an actress too?'

'Well, yes. Of course.'

'Wait there. I'll be back in a minute.'

Chilcott rushed back into the High-Tech Crime office.

'Can you remember what she was wearing when she came in to see us?' Chilcott asked Foster, who was still reviewing the CCTV footage.

'Not precisely. No.'

'But she had a long hooded black coat, did she not?'

'Yes, I think she did.'

'Long black hooded coat,' he said, pointing to the elusive selfie figure with her back to the camera and an arm around Travis Yardley's shoulder.

'That doesn't mean anything. That must be the most popular colour and style of coat at this time of year.'

'Look, Julie. Look at the evidence.' Chilcott kept his arm extended towards the screen.

Foster sighed. 'I don't know, Rob.'

'The hypnotist has just told me that she was an actress too – that he treated them both three years ago – that they carried around a pre-recording of his treatment for Yardley to use when he was on the road.'

Foster's eyes narrowed.

Chilcott turned to Deans. 'You were saying something at the crime scene. Say it again.'

'I'm sorry, sir?' DC Deans said.

'You were crouched down against the wall, and you kept saying something. What was it?'

Deans ran a hand through his hair and tilted his head back. 'Great again. I was saying great again.'

'Why? Why were you saying that?'

'It was what I was hearing in my head.' Deans turned away. 'I'm sorry, I can't explain it.'

'Male or female?'

'I'm sorry?'

'You heard a voice in your head. Was it male or female?'

Deans glanced at DCI Foster. 'It was female.'

'Tell me again what words the hypnotist uses to put Yardley under,' Foster asked McEwan.

'Make Travis great again.'

'And what did she say in the interview room?'

'Exactly those words, but with a whole lot of crocodile tears, just to add to the dramatic effect,' Chilcott said.

'Is the hypnotist still on the phone?'

'Yes, he is.'

The team followed Foster as she strode into the incident room.

'Is he on loudspeaker?'

'No.'

'McEwan,' she said, 'find a computer and look up if any of these claims are possible as I speak to him.'

'Yes, Ma'am.'

McEwan took a seat at a nearby desk and fired up the monitor.

Foster sat down behind the phone and hit the loud-speaker button.

'Hello.'

'This is outrageous. It's nearly—'

'My name is Detective Chief Inspector Julie Foster and I'm in charge of this investigation. I'm sorry you have been left holding on, but let me just clarify a few things with you if I may.'

'Oh, hello. Yes. Of course.'

'You have been able to hypnotise Travis Yardley with a pre-recorded message – yes?'

'It is preferable to conduct a two-way—'

'Yes, or no?'

'Uh… yes.'

'And if his wife had a recording stored on her phone of you giving that treatment, she could play it to Yardley and place him back in a hypnotic trance?'

'Technically, yes – but it would depend on his desire to want that therapy and on how relaxed he was.'

'Well, let me just run this scenario by you – last Saturday, you successfully hypnotised Travis Yardley remotely during a phone conversation before his show, following the planned treatment you both had. You were then unable to speak to him after the show, so you sent him a voicemail message bringing him out of his hypnosis.'

'That was the intention, yes.'

Foster looked across to McEwan, who nodded eagerly.

'Okay, imagine this scenario; what if his wife then played him the pre-recorded treatment, or a part of it almost immediately after being released from his hypnosis, placing him back into an altered state of consciousness... are you still with me?'

'Y–ess.'

'Is that possible?'

'Hmm. I would say it is possible, but the conditions would need to be right.'

'He would still be relaxed from your recent hypnosis, though would he not?'

'Yes, more than likely, if we are only talking about minutes.'

'We are.'

'Then yes. It is possible.'

'And the fact that you have hypnotised him numerous times, including remotely, would render him more susceptible?'

'Possibly.'

'Can I just pick on something?' Chilcott asked.

Foster leaned back, allowing Chilcott to move closer to the desk phone.

'A while back, you told me that hypnotists can't make someone do something against their will. Did I hear that right?'

'Yes. Absolutely.'

'So, you could tell Yardley to kill someone, but if his subconscious mind understood that to be wrong or against the law, even though he was hypnotised, he wouldn't go through with it?'

'Unless it was a desire that was already manifested within him, that's right.'

Chilcott and Foster stared at one another.

'Hypnosis is like a daydream,' the hypnotist said. 'We can all imagine that, I'm sure. We might be at work and think of ourselves having a pint in the pub garden or picking up a new car that we are excited about driving for the first time. We take ourselves to that place in those moments we drift off. And those thoughts are clear and vivid. That is the best way to describe hypnosis – like playing out a daydream.'

'Thank you,' Foster said. 'But what would it take for someone to kill if they were hypnotised?'

'Sometimes, when treating a patient for unpleasant memories that have taken control of their lives, we use abre-action to make that individual relive whatever traumatic event is holding them back. It's a potent technique but can release previously repressed emotion, including anger.'

'Opening Pandora's box?' Foster said.

'Something like that.'

'So, if Yardley was repressing unpleasant memories or emotions, it could trigger an adverse reaction from him?'

'Possibly, but I wasn't aware of any such history, and I haven't used that technique on Mr Yardley.'

'How about the death of his kids?' Chilcott said.

The hypnotist was silent.

'Did you know about that?'

'No. no, I didn't.'

'Don't you think that's something you should have known about?'

'Absolutely.'

'Can you think why Yardley didn't tell you?'

'Uh…I don't know. It has been around three years since I last worked with him.'

'Could his wife say something to him when he was hypnotised to trigger an abreaction?' Foster asked.

'Well, she would need to know what she was doing—'

'Let's just say, for argument's sake, she does.'

'I suppose it is possible.'

'Thank you. Sorry to wake you or keep you up at this late time. Your help has been very useful.'

Foster ended the call and sat motionless in the chair.

'I've been looking up what he's been saying, Ma'am. It's all there.'

'Thanks, Sean.'

'I remember watching a Derren Brown special on the TV,' McEwan continued. 'He made normal people commit a cash-in-transit robbery. Seeing the clips on the web just now reminded me about the show.'

'I seem to recall that.'

'Yes, Ma'am. It was brilliant. He used a phone call for his hypnotism.'

'Back to the here and now,' Chilcott said. 'We don't know what Coates may or may not have said in his ear about the kids. She's right there in his earhole; we even see her turn to face him as she's holding the phone. If she knows what she's doing, she could be unleashing those inner demons.'

'He said during his interview that she blames him,' Foster said. 'What if there is more to the deaths? What if he was somehow responsible?'

'Deliberately, you mean?'

'Yeah.'

Chilcott pouted as he considered the prospect.

'There's one person who will know.'

CHAPTER THIRTY-SEVEN

'Where is she staying?' DCI Foster asked Chilcott.

'We put her up in the Premier Inn down on King Street.'

Foster looked at her watch. 'It's nearly ten-to-midnight. Get a car. We're going down there.'

When they arrived, they found the front doors locked to the public. Chilcott pressed the intercom, and an Eastern European voice answered after what seemed like ages.

'Hello,' he said. 'This is the police. We need to gain entry, please.'

The line crackled, and the voice came back.

'Hello. Can I help you?'

Chilcott rolled his eyes and stepped so close to the intercom microphone he looked like he was kissing or licking it.

'We are the police. Let us inside the door, please.'

The small silver box crackled again.

'Is he going to let us in or what?' Chilcott fumed.

'Calm yourself.'

'Calm? Bloody calm?'

Just as Chilcott was about to let rip, a young drunken couple approached them and walked directly for the door.

'Aww, you couldn't do us a favour, could you, guys?' Chilcott said. 'We've left our keys in the room and can't get in.'

'No worries,' one of the young men said, using his plastic card to release the door latch.

Chilcott pulled the door wide for the entwined couple to walk through, and they filed in close behind. The young man dabbed his card on another electronic door lock as he kissed his partner, and they continued walking on without so much as a second look back.

The reception desk was empty of staff with the appearance of a typical affordable-budget affair; a crescent-shaped desk with a tourist flyer display at the side containing brochures and leaflets for local excursions and places of interest.

Chilcott leaned over the desk. 'Hello,' he called out. He tried to look around the wall, but it blocked the view from the reception desk. These hotel designers weren't stupid.

'Hello,' he called out again, but nobody came.

DCI Foster straight-armed Chilcott and ushered him gently back away from the desk.

'Excuse me…' she called out, and almost immediately, a face appeared from behind the side wall.

Foster gave Chilcott a *fifteen–love* twitch of the brow and engaged the gentleman behind the desk.

'Good evening,' she said. 'My name is Detective Chief Inspector Julie Foster, and these are my colleagues.'

The receptionist gawped at the five detectives, who were pretty much taking up the entire space of the foyer.

'We were let in by one of your patrons,' Foster smiled.

The man continued eyeing the group of suit-clad detectives and simply uttered, 'Okay.'

'We are interested to know which room a young lady is staying in who we need to speak to urgently.'

'Okay,' the man said timidly.

'Mrs Georgia Coates.'

Foster gave the young man a warm smile.

'I'm not sure I can—'

'You can, son,' Chilcott cut in. 'Let's put it another way. We're not leaving here until you show us to her room.'

Foster turned to Chilcott and gave him a disapproving scowl.

'I'm sorry,' she said. 'We've all had quite a long day, and our patience is wearing a little thin.'

Chilcott huffed behind her back.

'Okay, let me take a quick look,' the man said.

'Are you on your own tonight?' Foster asked him.

'Always on my own at nights,' he replied flatly.

'Have you got a TV or something in the backroom to keep you entertained?'

The man rocked his head, neither agreeing nor disagreeing with the question.

'No. No name,' he said.

'I'm sorry,' Foster said, leaning over the desk.

'No, George Coates.'

'Not George,' Chilcott said. 'Georgia. Mrs. A woman.'

He noticed Foster giving him a dirty stare, so he stepped back into her shadows and out of her firing range.

'That's what I said, innit? No Georgia Coates.'

'Um, I'm sorry, but there must be,' Foster said. 'Avon and Somerset Police are paying for the room. Perhaps it's booked under that name instead?'

The man clicked a couple of buttons and shook his head. 'No. Not here.'

'She came down this morning. She's only staying for—'

'No, she's not,' Julie,' Chilcott said. 'She was in the area on Saturday night. She's been here all bloody week – making sure Yardley doesn't get released from custody.'

'Why' Foster asked Chilcott bluntly.

They were all back in the incident room. All tired. All dejected.

'Why would Georgia Coates go to the vast trouble of putting Travis Yardley through all this?'

'Because she blames him for the death of their children.'

'Has that been verified?'

Chilcott took a report from DC Fowler's hand.

'Deans was right,' he sighed. 'We should have checked against Yardley's real name. Amy has done some digging and found this report from Police Scotland. We didn't have anything on our systems because the Scottish and English databases don't talk to one another unless specifically requested.'

'Let me see that,' Foster said, taking the report from Chilcott.

She read through it and puffed out air. 'Good work, Amy.' She looked at Deans. 'Good work, Andy. They did well to keep this out of the public arena.'

'There was nothing about it at all on the search engines Ma'am.'

'That's incredible. So where does this leave us now?'

'With about three hundred hotels and B and Bs to check before Coates buggers off,' Chilcott said.

Foster wiped her face. 'There must be an easier way?'

'Her phone, Ma'am?' DC Fowler suggested.

'Go on.'

'We could run a check against her number. Triangulate the position and see what pings?'

Foster looked sideways at Chilcott, who jiggled a shoulder.

'It's not really the done thing, Amy,' Foster said. 'We need to consider the Regulation of Investigatory Powers Act.'

'I think it's a good shout,' Chilcott said. 'We can justify our actions as far as RIPA goes. After all, we are viewing Georgia Coates for incitement to commit murder.'

DCI Foster considered the suggestion for a moment. 'Okay,' she said. 'Put in an urgent request to triangulate against Georgia Coates' phone number since last Saturday. Let's see where she's been going, and perhaps, we can narrow it down to a part of the city where we can concentrate our efforts. How long will that take?'

'It would normally be twenty-four hours for a full report, Ma'am,' DC Fowler said.

'We haven't got twenty-four hours.' Foster looked at her watch. 'We've got just under fifteen and half hours before Yardley's custody clock runs out.'

'Leave it with me,' Chilcott said. 'I can be pretty persuasive when needs must.'

'Why don't we just call her,' DC Deans said. 'We could tell her that we need to talk to her again; tell her something has happened with Yardley overnight.'

They all looked at him.

'Mrs Coates said that she'll do anything to help him out. She needs to keep up that pretence, even if it's not the true reason why she's here. We can still get the triangulation authority, and when we call her, we can see where she is in real-time. We won't have to wait for the report. There will be no guess work. It'll be in our faces. If she doesn't turn up at the place and time we stipulate, which I suspect she will, then we can visit each of the hotels within the range of the mobile phone triangulation.'

Foster smiled. 'I like it. Fine. The rest of you go home apart from DI Chilcott and me. We're going to send off for this authorisation, so we've got it in the morning. Get some sleep and be back here at 6 a.m. It's going to be an interesting day.'

CHAPTER THIRTY-EIGHT

Thursday 10th March

7:26 a.m.

Chilcott didn't like taking his foot off the gas when he knew time was of the essence. There was a fine line between burning the midnight oil and simply burning out. But yesterday had been a tough one to take, and he had managed to sleep for about three hours. He looked around the room at the small team riding his wave. They had gelled well, each of them bringing something different to the investigation. That was what made his job so great – seeing the invention and dedication from his team.

He lingered on Deans. They wouldn't even be in this position if it wasn't for him. Short of the victims and crime scene, Yardley would be released without charge. But for now, Chilcott's sights were solely fixed on adding Georgia Coates to the charge sheet.

They were inside the DCI's office. The same small team who had been there just hours before, except for DC Fowler who was logged onto the telecoms tracking system. Foster had the phone on loudspeaker, and they were all silently waiting for Georgia Coates to respond.

'Hello,' came the weary reply.

'Good morning, Mrs Coates. This is DCI Foster. I'm sorry for the early call, but I wanted to catch you before you jumped on the train.'

'Is everything okay?'

'Actually, no, it's not.'

'Oh. What's going on?'

'Travis has had an accident.'

'An accident?'

Chilcott dropped Foster a look of shock, and she scowled back.

'I'd prefer not to talk about it on the phone,' Foster said. 'Can we meet you at the Premier Inn?'

'No. No, I'll come to you. Are you with Travis?'

'No. We're at the office at the moment, but we could pick you up if you like?'

'No, it's okay. I'll get a taxi. You've done enough for me already.'

Foster looked out of the glass walls of her office at DC Fowler, who gave a thumbs-up.

'Okay, it's almost seven-thirty now, shall we say eight or eight-thirty. Does that give you enough time to get ready?'

'Sure.'

'What time is checkout? Perhaps we should say nine and

then you can bring your bags with you. We can sort you out with transport afterwards. That's not a problem.'

'Ah, yes. Okay. I'll see you at nine at your station.'

'Good. We'll talk properly then. Goodbye.'

'Bye.'

The call ended, and Foster sank back into her chair.

'I can't believe how well you lie,' Chilcott said to her.

'It's not in my nature. I didn't know what else to say?'

'Shall we see where she is?'

'Come on,' Foster said, standing up. 'Let's see what Amy has discovered.'

They all left the DCI's office and surrounded DC Fowler's desk.

'What have we got, Amy?' Foster said.

'There are over a thousand masts in Bristol, Ma'am.'

'Really?'

'But because of that, we've got a pretty narrow triangulation here.' She pointed to the screen. 'Queen Square.'

'Queen Square – that's near the Premier Inn.'

'Yes, and looking at the map, there are another five or six hotels and hostels in that segment, as well as the Premier Inn.'

'Can we narrow those down at all?'

'Not really, Ma'am.'

Chilcott leaned into the screen. 'She didn't strike me as a Youth Hostel kind of woman, so I think we can scrub that one from the list. And there's another hostel. Get rid of that one too.'

'I think she'd be here,' Foster said, pointing to a hotel on the Quayside. 'I've been there. It's nice.'

'When did you stay there?' Chilcott asked Foster.

'I didn't stay there. I had a meal if you must know.'

'Who with?'

Foster raked her head and stared for a long moment at Chilcott. 'I don't think we need to discuss my social habits right here, right now.'

'I was just asking. No need to bite my head off.' Chilcott scuffed his heels on the floor and continued mumbling, 'If you don't want to tell us who you were on a date with, that's fine with me.'

'It wasn't a date.'

Chilcott raised a hand. 'Okay, that's fine. It wasn't a date with this secret person.'

'Robbie.' Foster had a spiky look on her face. 'Can we please just continue with this? I'm not rising to your bait, no matter how hard you try.'

'No. That's fine,' he said playfully, looking away. 'You keep your secrets safe.' He smiled and looked back at her. 'I'll get it out of you later.'

'Can we just carry on with the task in hand, please, Robbie?'

Chilcott raised his palms in submission. 'You're the boss.'

'Yes, I am. Now, here's what we'll do – the rest of the team arrives at eight. I want Sean and Amy to tie up with another officer, and then you all head down to the hotel we've identified. Don't go inside, but hover somewhere close by. One of us will call you from here if Georgia Coates turns up. We'll then go in under a Section 18 warrant and search her hotel room once she's been arrested. You guys will seize any phones or recording equipment that might have evidence relating to the hypnotist's treatment. Is that clear?'

'Yes, Ma'am,' DCs Fowler and McEwan said together.'

'What about Deans?' Chilcott said.

'I want Andy here with us.'

'Yes, Ma'am,' Deans said.

'We will then transport Coates to custody and see what we get from her in the interview.'

CHAPTER THIRTY-NINE

9:07 a.m.

Chilcott prowled like a caged animal.

'How much longer do we give it?' he said. 'She's only gone and bloody seen us off.'

'Hold on,' Foster said. 'Let's give it a few more minutes before we panic.'

'I'm not panicking, but we've only got seven hours until Yardley's custody clock runs out.'

'I know we've only got seven hours.'

The desk phone rang, and Foster picked it up. It was the reception on the ground floor. Foster had a visitor.

'She's here,' Foster said. 'Andy, I want you to go with Robbie. Meet her in reception and take her into the side room. Robbie, you arrest her on suspicion of incitement to commit murder.'

'Why me?'

'Because Andy is a visiting DC. This needs to be

handled internally. I want this process as streamlined as possible.'

'Okay,' Chilcott grumbled.

'I'm sure Andy can remind you of the words of the caution if it has been a while?'

'Haha, very funny. No, I think I can just about remember the lines, thank you.'

'We'll need a female officer to go with you.'

'No problem. I'll take someone from the office. Penny Chiba will be ideal —she's had a lot of input in the case already.'

'Let me know as soon as Coates is arrested, and I'll make my way to Keynsham separately.'

'You're not worried about Yardley and Coates being in the same custody centre?' Chilcott asked.

'No. We'll put her in a separate wing away from where Yardley is housed. He won't even know she's there. And we can't afford the time to travel between two custody centres. Let's keep this simple. Let's get the job done and get them both charged.'

Mrs Coates smiled at seeing Chilcott and the others enter the main reception area.

'Mrs Coates,' Chilcott said. 'Thanks for coming over.'

'That's no problem at all. Anything to help Travis.'

'Yes, I bet.' Chilcott gave her a broad grin. 'Can we just go in here a moment, please,' he said, pushing a side door open into a small private meeting room.

'Of course,' Mrs Coates said, giving Deans and Chiba a quick once-over.

They all stepped inside, and Chilcott closed the door. Mrs Coates moved for a chair.

'Uh, we don't need to sit down. This won't take long.'

'Oh, okay.'

Chilcott moved forward, and Deans automatically covered the space vacated beside the exit.

'Mrs Coates,' Chilcott said, looking down at his wrist watch. 'It's now nine sixteen in the morning. I am arresting you on suspicion of incitement to commit murder.' He took an extra step to close the gap between them further.

'What?' Mrs Coates said, looking at the three detectives with frantic urgency.

'You do not have to say anything, but it may harm your defence if you do not mention when questioned something you later rely upon in court. And anything you do say may be given in evidence. Do you understand?'

Mrs Coates edged backwards.

'My colleague, DC Chiba, is going to search you now. Do you have anything sharp on you?'

'What? No, of course not... I'm sorry. What's happening. I don't understand?'

DC Chiba came forwards and instructed Mrs Coates to keep her arms out to the side. She began patting down her pockets and removed a mobile phone from her jacket.

'We'll have that, thank you, Mrs Coates,' Chilcott said.

'What? Why are you doing this? I haven't done anything wrong.' She tugged her arm away from DC Chiba, who pulled it back with equal force.

'Stand still,' DC Chiba said firmly. 'I'll tell you when you can move.'

Mrs Coates glowered at Penny Chiba for a fleeting

second and then stared at Chilcott. Her eyes were starting to pool with tears.

'Mrs Coates, as soon as we are satisfied that you are safe to transport, we are taking you to a custody centre where you will be interviewed under caution.'

Her eyes were wide and incredulous. 'For what?'

'Incitement to commit murder, Mrs Coates.'

'I... wha—?'

'All clear,' DC Chiba said.

'We are going to seize your phone as evidence, Mrs Coates. And we will look after your other possessions, just while you are with us.'

'No,' she said, tugging her arm away again.

'Slap the bangles on, Penny,' Chilcott said to DC Chiba, noticing Mrs Coates searching beyond his shoulder for the door behind him.

'Why are you doing this? You have no right to treat me this way.'

'We are exercising our powers afforded to us by the Police and Criminal Evidence Act of nineteen eighty-four, following suspicion of a criminal offence. We are merely affecting a prompt and effective investigation, Mrs Coates. And we have every right to detain you.'

Chilcott turned to Deans. 'Right, let's go.'

DC Deans opened the door, and they escorted Mrs Coates back out through the foyer and directly to a waiting unmarked police vehicle outside.

CHAPTER FORTY

Mrs Coates declined to be legally represented during her interview, as was her legal choice. It didn't bother Chilcott unduly, so long as he and his colleagues did everything that followed strictly by the book, it didn't matter what she said if anything at all. They sat opposite one another, Mrs Coates with the appearance of an innocent child summoned to the headmaster's office for something she didn't do, and Chilcott and DC Chiba, arms folded, faces glumly evaluating their subject.

'You've made a mistake,' Mrs Coates said. 'I… I really don't know why I'm here?'

'I've told you three times now why you are here,' Chilcott said.

'But you're wrong.'

She whined and sobbed loudly into a paper tissue supplied to her by DC Chiba.

'Tell us about Saturday night,' Chilcott said, his arms still firmly planted across his chest.

'I, uh… like what?'

'Like where were you?'

She shook her head. 'I don't know, at home, I suppose.'

'Alone?'

She instinctively clawed at the side of her head. 'No… I… I was with my girls.'

Chilcott squinted.

'Doing what, exactly?'

'Uh…watching TV, cuddling up… stuff like that.'

'What were you watching?'

She peered at Chilcott for a half-second. 'At what time?'

'Let's say 8 p.m. for starters, shall we.'

Her eyes flicked away, then immediately returned to Chilcott's face.

'I was watching a film on *Netflix*.'

'Which one?'

She scowled and laughed at the same time. 'I don't understand why you need to know this?' She lifted her body weight from the chair and repositioned herself back down at an angle with her knees pointing towards the door.

Chilcott picked up on the subtle gesture. She wanted to leave the room.

'Which one?' he repeated.

'I don't like the way you are talking to me.'

Chilcott blinked. 'Tough luck.'

'I beg your pardon.'

Mrs Coates dabbed a finger beneath her eyes – one after the other – even though Chilcott could see she wasn't crying.

He cocked his head and watched her for a considered moment.

'I want to see my husband,' she said. 'Now – I want to see him right now.'

'Ex... husband, Mrs Coates. You are separated, remember?'

'Oh, for God's sake.'

Chilcott slowly unravelled his arms and gently interlocked his fingers, resting his hands on the desk in front of him.

'Well, aren't you going to ask me something else?'

Chilcott ran the tip of his tongue around the inside edge of his top lip, not taking his eyes from his subject.

'Which film?' he said again.

'Why must you know what sodding film I watched?'

Chilcott's face softened. 'I'd like to know if it's something I've seen myself.'

'What?'

'Denzel Washington,' Chilcott said.

'What?' Mrs Coates said again. Her voice was getting higher. 'What are you talking about?'

Chilcott unclasped his hands and rubbed his forehead repeatedly as if soothing away a building headache. He closed his eyes as the massage took effect, and he made Mrs Coates wait until he was finished.

He sucked in deeply and held it for a long second. 'My favourite actor,' he said, emptying his lungs again.

'What?' Mrs Coates whispered. Her face was tight and questioning.

Chilcott dipped his head and looked at her from beneath the hood of his lids.

'Denzel is my favourite actor. Who's yours?'

'Uh... what? Uh... I don't know... Meryl Streep,

probably?'

'Good choice. Great actress. Very plausible.' He left the words hanging somewhere between them.

She twitched her head and glimpsed DC Chiba. 'Doesn't he let you talk?'

'When I need to,' DC Chiba responded flatly.

Mrs Coates huffed with evident frustration.

'Tell us about Saturday night,' Chilcott asked again.

Mrs Coates shot him a fierce glare. 'I just did, and this is breaching my human rights.'

Chilcott scratched at his chin and pushed himself up in his chair. He pointed his finger towards her. 'That's a good one,' he said. 'Human rights…'

She scowled, blinking, and looked between Chilcott and Chiba, but neither of them spoke.

'This is nothing short of police brutality,' she fired at them both.

Chilcott laughed behind closed lips and gently bounced his weight against the plastic back of his chair.

Mrs Coates shook her head, and her salon-fresh hair wobbled.

'Well, ask me something,' she said. 'I've got a home to get to.'

Chilcott turned his head towards DC Chiba for the first time since they had started the interview. 'She says she's got a home to get to,' he said as if DC Chiba hadn't heard the comment.

DC Chiba replied with a grunt.

Mrs Coates planted her hands down flat on the table. 'I have to go. I've got my girls—'

'No, you don't.'

Mrs Coates raised herself up from the chair.

'Sit down,' Chilcott said softly.

'I'm not listening to any more of this nonsense. I'm going. I've got a train to catch.' She stood up away from the chair and made swiftly towards the door.

'I said. Sit down.'

Coates continued onwards.

'We know all about you,' Chilcott said, swivelling in his seat before she reached the door.

Mrs Coates stopped in her tracks, a foot from the exit. She didn't turn around and continued facing ahead.

'We know you were in Bath on Saturday night.'

Mrs Coates remained motionless.

'We know you weren't at your parents' house in St Albans, and we know you haven't been staying at the Premier Inn.' He waited five seconds. 'We know you saw Travis outside of the theatre after the show on Saturday night, and we know you showed him something on your phone that put him into a dangerous state of hypnosis.'

He saw her shoulders starting to lift and drop as her breathing intensified.

'We know you showed him a video clip of his hypnotist's treatment. We know you put him back into hypnosis.'

Mrs Coates didn't try to turn around.

'We also know you didn't watch TV with your girls.'

Chilcott paused just long enough for the following words to have maximum impact.

'We know they are dead... and so are your parents—'

She turned; her teeth bared, and made a desperate lunge for Chilcott, her arms thrashing wildly as she came at him.

'You fucking bastard,' she screamed. 'You fucking bastard.'

Chilcott dipped a shoulder, and she caught him a glancing blow with her fingers, just as DC Chiba smashed into her from a side angle, forcing them both off balance and into a sprawling mass on the floor.

'He locked them in,' Mrs Coates screamed uncontrollably. 'He locked them inside because they were getting in the way of his fame.' She thrashed wildly as DC Chiba did her best to contain her rabid attempts to get back on her feet. 'He took away everything I loved,' she bellowed. 'He deserves to rot in hell for what he's done.'

Chilcott stood up from his chair and straightened his jacket as DC Chiba wrestled on the floor with the wildly-determined Mrs Coates, who was shrieking and spitting like a ferocious animal. He pressed the thin panic strip that ran around the perimeter of the interview room, and almost instantaneously, the door burst open and three, then four, and then five officers rushed in to control Mrs Coates on the floor.

Chilcott moved aside and readjusted his tie as he watched on with considered interest as Mrs Coates continued to shout, swear and lash out in Chilcott's direction.

DC Chiba pulled herself up from the floor and stood back as the detention officers took control of the situation. Her long black hair was dangling across her face.

'You okay, Pen?'

'Yes, thanks,' she panted. 'Are you okay, boss?'

She stared at his face. 'You're bleeding.'

'Am I?' He dabbed a hand on the side of his cheek and saw a wet smear of blood across his fingers. 'Oh, bugger.'

'She caught you good and proper, sir,' DC Chiba said. 'Just as well I was here – who knows what might have happened otherwise?'

'Yeah, thanks, Pen. Just remind me not to get on your wrong side in the future, will you.'

DC Chiba smiled and handed Chilcott a paper tissue from the table.

'You'll need this.'

'Thanks.'

'My dad made me take up martial arts when I was a kid,' she said. 'It comes in handy occasionally.'

Chilcott dabbed his face. 'Yeah. I can see that was a youth well spent.'

His phone vibrated in his pocket, and he took it out to look.

Hello Robbie, I hope you are still okay to meet in London? Call me. Bette xx

He felt his cheeks glowing at the mere thought of seeing his French colleague again.

'Everything okay, sir?' DC Chiba asked him.

'Me? Oh, yes… I'm fine… I'm fine.'

'Are you sure, sir?'

'Why do you ask,' he said, stuffing the phone back into his pocket.

'You look like you've just had a shock, that's all, sir.'

He blinked. He *was* shocked. He was shocked Bette had the slightest interest in him. He looked at his watch. 'Come on, Penny. Let's update the DCI and see if we can get these two on the charge sheet before we're too late.'

CHAPTER FORTY-ONE

12:42 p.m.

Foster and Chilcott watched through the glass walls of his office as DC McEwan spoke on the phone to the CPS lawyer about the strengths and weaknesses of the case. The CPS would have the final decision if or how Yardley and his ex-wife would be charged. McEwan was already forty minutes into the call, and his cheeks were as flushed as his pink shirt.

'This is by no means a done deal,' Foster said.

Chilcott swung gently on his chair. 'McEwan's a good kid. He'll get it done.'

'It's not about McEwan – it's this case. I wouldn't be surprised if it went either way.'

Chilcott sniffed.

'Think about it,' Foster said. 'Yardley kills those two victims, but he was in an altered state of consciousness. He entered into a contract while on stage, but not afterwards in the street. We come back to the suggestion of involuntary automatism, and some would argue that he is a victim too.'

'Not if he's got badness running through him.'

'We won't know that for sure until we get our hands on the coroner's report from Police Scotland. If those kids and their grandparents were locked inside the home intentionally and there is the slightest suggestion the fire was started deliberately, then he's in a sticky situation.'

'They obviously didn't think there was enough evidence at the time, or else they'd have charged him.'

Foster nodded.

'I can't help thinking about what the hypnotist said, though. Even in hypnosis, a person still has free will. That blows the involuntary automatism argument out of the water.'

'Maybe.'

'Anyway, you've got nothing to worry about. It's not you stood in court if these two jokers get charged.'

Foster turned to Chilcott. 'It's not like you to worry about a court case. This one will be headline news.

'Exactly! A crime is committed by a famous actor hypnotised against his will, and a psychic detective discovers the victims. What could possibly go wrong? The headline writers will have a field day with this one.'

'Now you come to mention it…'

'Thanks for your support.'

'You're welcome.'

DC McEwan slammed the receiver down with a triumphant fist pump in the air.

'We've got it, boss,' he shouted. 'Two charges of murder

for Yardley and a charge of incitement to commit murder for Coates.'

Chilcott acknowledged McEwan with a thumbs-up.

'Good work, Robbie,' Foster said.

'Why do I think this will come back and bite me in the arse in ten months?'

'Stop worrying about the court case and go and give the troops a pat on the back. I'll notify the chief we've got a result.'

Chilcott left his office and joined his team in the incident room.

'Good work, everyone. Good work. Sean, get the charges built and go and do the honours, son.'

'Cheers, boss.'

McEwan skipped off, high-fiving DC Fowler and DC Chiba as he breezed out of the office.

Chilcott stayed where he was, perched on the edge of a desk. Deep in his thoughts.

'I guess that's me done then, sir,' DC Deans said, striding across to Chilcott.

'I suppose it is.'

Chilcott held out his hand, and Deans shook it. Chilcott didn't let go, and he stared at the enigmatic detective for a meaningful minute.

'This is your victory, son,' he said. 'We wouldn't have got that charging decision without your input. Yardley would be walking, and two dead people would still be there, undiscovered. They would be found, eventually, but that's not the point. Because of you, we beat the clock, and we got Yardley on the charge sheet.'

Deans rolled his head. 'You would have found them, sir – even without me.'

'No. I wouldn't.' He turned away. 'And that makes me realise a few things about myself that I don't necessarily like.'

'None of this is a game, though, sir.'

'No,' Chilcott agreed in a whisper. 'But sometimes we must find a way to keep on going through the horrors of human-kind, and turning it into something tangible helps me deal with it.'

Deans looked around Chilcott's face for a long moment and took an edge of the table next to him. He looked out into the room. 'So, this is what a murder squad looks like.'

Chilcott smiled.

'Someone like you could be useful in a place like this.'

'Nah. I'm a small city boy. Always have been, always will be.'

Chilcott silently mulled over the events of the last few days.

'I still don't understand how you did it?'

Deans cocked his head and looked away. 'I was the same. I didn't believe or want to believe the signals and messages that were in plain sight.' He sighed. 'If I'm honest, I still don't.'

Chilcott creased his brow.

'I don't know what tomorrow will bring, or the next day? All I know is, at some point, I will see, feel, hear, smell or taste… death. I'm not sure that's something worth celebrating.'

Chilcott watched Deans with a measured eye. Maybe they weren't that different after all?

Deans sprang himself from the edge of the desk and stood in front of Chilcott. 'I'll see you around, sir.' He kept on staring at Chilcott.

'What is it, son?'

'Make the most of the time you have, sir. The here – the now. Cherish the small moments. Soak up the good times. And never let them be smothered in your memories by the bad. Life is short, precious and precarious, with only one sure eventuality – you'll leave people behind who will miss you desperately. Love and be loved, and you won't go far wrong, even in the worst of times.'

'That's a bit deep for me, son.'

Deans smiled and winked. 'No, it's not. Enjoy your special weekend.'

He smiled again and walked towards the exit.

Chilcott watched him as the rest of the team bode him farewell.

As those final words played out again in his head, he now realised what Deans was talking about, and at that moment, he finally made up his mind; he did like Deans.

Occasionally in life, you meet someone who radiates everything good about mankind. I was lucky enough to serve alongside such a man, who I was proud to call one of my very best friends. This book is also dedicated to Mike Magee and the many loved ones he leaves behind.

In loving memory of PC 2794 Mike Magee.

FREE EBOOK

Would you like to learn more about Detective Deans and how he developed his extraordinary abilities?

For the first time, *STORM LOG-0505* is free to download direct from my website.

Visit www.jamesdmortain.com to find out more and download your free full-length novel.

THE DETECTIVE DEANS MYSTERY SERIES

STORM LOG-0505
eBook/Paperback/Audio

DEAD BY DESIGN
eBook/Paperback/Audio

THE BONE HILL
eBook/Paperback/Audio

THE DI CHILCOTT MYSTERY SERIES

DEAD RINGER
eBook/Paperback/Audio

DEATH DO US PART
eBook/Paperback/Audio

A WHISPER OF EVIL
eBook/Paperback/*Audio - coming soon!*

ACKNOWLEDGMENTS

I had a difficult time writing this book. I lost a close friend, and I couldn't motivate myself to write. Soon after, I discovered my aunt was terminally ill and had just days to live. She asked me to call her, and she told me that she had recently picked up a copy of Storm Log-0505 and enjoyed it - so much so she had told her neighbours about the book and shared passages with her Reverend - I can only hope they were appropriate! My aunt was so positive and utterly inspirational, and she made me promise her that I would continue writing stories. And so, the biggest thanks for this book goes to dear aunt Edna. I also extend a sincere thank you to Mike's family for allowing me to pay my respects to my friend in this book.

I wish to say a big thank you to my fabulous editor, Debz Hobbs-Wyatt. To my trusted advisers: Phil Croll, Terry Galbraith, Heidi Miller, Liz Wheeler, and Rachael. Thank you for taking the time to share your knowledge and creative ideas with me.

I am hugely grateful to my advanced reader team who pick up the flaws that slip through the net. You are the best!

To those who have allowed me to use their real names as characters; Julie Foster, Fleur Phillips, Nathan Parsons, Richard Allen, Penny Fleming and Emily Chiba (who make up DC Penny Chiba), Melanie Sellars and my old mate Harvey Samways - thanks so much!

Finally, a sincere thank you to my growing band of readers and reviewers. Some of you have been with me since the very start, and I hope you come back for more!

Visit www.jamesdmortain.com to grab a freebie, or if you would like to join my amazing advanced reader team.

ABOUT THE AUTHOR

Photograph Copyright of Mick Kavanagh Photography.

Former British CID Detective turned crime fiction writer James brings thrilling action and gritty authenticity to his writing through years of police experience. Originally from Bath, England, James now lives in North Devon with his young family.

James has a 'normal' day job, he is also a content writer for a luxury travel company, but is happiest creating fictional mystery and mayhem. Don't miss the latest releases by following James on Amazon, Bookbub and Goodreads.

You can connect with James on social media or here on his website: www.jamesdmortain.com

Please send any emails to jdm@manverspublishing.com.

facebook.com/jamesdmortain

twitter.com/@jamesdmortain

instagram.com/jamesmortain